W9-AJQ-693

3 4028 08508 4805
HARRIS COUNTY PUBLIC LIBRARY

YA Moore
Moore, Stephanie Perry
Truth and nothing but

DISCARD

$7.95
ocn867024470
10/14/2014

Truth and Nothing But

THE **SHARP** SISTERS

#4
Truth and Nothing But

STEPHANIE PERRY MOORE

darbycreek
MINNEAPOLIS

Text copyright © 2014 by Stephanie Perry Moore

All rights reserved. International copyright secured. No part of this book may be reproduced, stored in a retrieval system, or transmitted in any form or by any means—electronic, mechanical, photocopying, recording, or otherwise—without the prior written permission of Lerner Publishing Group, Inc., except for the inclusion of brief quotations in an acknowledged review.

Darby Creek
A division of Lerner Publishing Group, Inc.
241 First Avenue North
Minneapolis, MN 55401 USA

For reading levels and more information, look up this title at www.lernerbooks.com.

The images in this book are used with the permission of:
Front cover: © R. Gino Santa Maria/Shutterstock.com; SeanPavone Photo/Shutterstock.com (background).

Main body text set in Janson Text LT Std 12/17.5.
Typeface provided by Linotype AG.

Library of Congress Cataloging-in-Publication Data

Moore, Stephanie Perry.
      Truth and nothing but / by Stephanie Perry Moore.
         pages cm. — (The Sharp sisters; #4)
      Summary: "Sloan is the youngest of Stanley Sharp's daughters and her dream is to be a reporter. She soon discovers learning the truth is harder than she imagined."— Provided by publisher.
      ISBN 978-1-4677-3727-2 (lib. bdg. : alk. paper)
      ISBN 978-1-4677-4658-8 (eBook)
      [1. Sisters—Fiction. 2. Journalism—Fiction. 3. Scandals—Fiction.
4. African Americans—Fiction] I. Title.
      PZ7.M788125Ts 2014
      [Fic]—dc23   2013048213

Manufactured in the United States of America
1 – SB – 7/15/14

For
Maya Angelou

Thank you for teaching me why the
caged bird sings.
Your writings have inspired many black
girls to fly.
I have been working over the years to
do the same with my prose.
You leave a mark that makes us all dig
and find the truth inside us.
May every person reading this series
want to leave as strong a legacy.

You are a hero of mine. Blessed
you have shown me the way…
keep soaring!

CHAPTER ONE
SPIRIT

We all may think Stanley Sharp is sterling clean as the front-runner in the mayoral race. However, stay tuned for some dirty facts that prove he is far from polished. Those were the notes written by a reporter who happened to be sitting next to me.

I didn't know the man, but on the top of the paper was the name Schultz. He was standing kitty-corner away from me, talking to a female reporter. I wondered why this man had it in for my dad.

I was supposed to be overly excited. This was Sloan Ann Sharp's time to learn and grow. I was rubbing elbows with the city's best reporters. Since I was five, I knew I wanted to be a journalist, so this opportunity to be near the best journalists in my area was a dream come true.

All the Sharp girls were dreamers. I was my dad's fourth of five girls. Actually, I was the biological youngest. My parents had adopted two of the five of us. Yuri, one of the adopted sisters, was a day younger than me. Ansli and Yuri were gorgeous mixed beauties who lost their parents when we were all young. Yuri, who was also my best friend, loved baking. Shelby, the fashionista, was the oldest daughter and two years older than me. Slade, the songstress, was only a year older than me. Ansli, who was the same age as Shelby, took award-winning photos.

All five of us were basically our own crew. For the last year, we'd been our father's shadows, escorting him all around town. Though we girls had been in his corner, our strong mother really had his back.

Campaigns get messy, and this one was no different. We were tired of being in the spotlight. Thankfully, we were all at the last mayoral debate. My father was leading the race to run the city of Charlotte, and all the polls were saying in a few days he'd be crowned the winner.

But how could I stay excited when the reporters were fishing for foolishness to make him look bad? It took everything in me to refrain from going to that Mr. Schultz and giving him a piece of my mind. See, I wasn't like the rest of my sisters. They were all refined, sweet, and nice. They said what was supposed to be said and didn't buck the system. I, however, didn't like it when adults played me. I believed I had as much worth as anyone, even though I might not have been on the earth as long.

I knew I wanted to be a writer, but not of novels or anything trivial. I wanted to win the Pulitzer Prize for my work. I had a deep longing to cover stories that would make the world better. Covering this debate was my opportunity to start. Our school, Marks High School, was just starting this year, so we were developing a newspaper. The first edition was supposed to hold my published work. Because I had press credentials, I wasn't sitting with my family at the debate. I was getting an up-front, first-class seat to report on the debate from a student's perspective. If my teacher approved my entry, it was going to get published.

My sister Shelby wasn't as outspoken as I was, but she didn't bite her tongue. She came up to me, leaned in, and said, "You sitting here with your mouth all hung open, looking all stank and stuff. Don't be representing the family any ol' kind of way."

I wanted to tell her, "You don't even have all the information. If you saw what I saw, that someone was about to tell lies on our father, you'd be just as mad as I am." But until I investigated and knew what was real, I wasn't going to spread lies. Trying to keep Shelby in check, I gave her a fake smile. She patted me on the head, like I was some good dog she was proud of. I didn't get mad though. Shelby and I were cool. I understood her brashness; I had more of it than she did. When the debate was about to start, she went to go sit down with my mom and sisters.

An hour later, the debate was still going on. I was a little tired of the bull I felt the candidates were giving. Even tons of promises were coming from my father. No way was all they were saying possible to achieve. Everyone was trying to make himself look stellar. They should, but as a reporter, I had to see through the bull and report the truth.

There were only a few questions left. While I thought my dad was overselling himself a bit, he was getting loud cheers and claps after every question. Out of the three candidates, my dad was still the best choice. The other two sometimes weren't even answering the questions but were using their microphone time to beg for votes.

When the moderator turned to the press section and asked if there were any questions, Mr. Schultz beside me stood up and was handed the mic. "I'd like to ask this question to Mr. Sharp."

"Certainly, Mr. Schultz, go right ahead," my dad said, showing all his pearly whites.

"There have been a lot of scandals with

public figures in the recent decade. Even the two gentlemen running against you have been under severe scrutiny. One questioned for domestic violence, the other under tax investigation."

"And do you have a question, Mr. Schultz?" my dad asked, as his wide smile was waning.

"I'm getting to that, sir."

Under my breath I said, "Well, get to the question then, jerk."

Suddenly, I realized that maybe Mr. Schultz wanted to trap my dad and ask him something about this so-called scandal that was written on the notepad. Immediately, I started coughing. No one was noticing, so I coughed louder.

A female reporter who was sitting beside Mr. Schultz reached over his empty chair and gave me her unopened bottle of water. "Take this, honey."

I nodded thanks. I had to take a sip even though I was fine. She smiled, pleased I was now quiet.

Mr. Schultz saw I was taken care of and asked his question. "Do you think an elected official needs to come clean to the constituents who vote him in?"

"I'm not sure if I fully understand your question."

"Is that because you've got something to hide?"

"Okay, you're making a lot of assumptions there, Mr. Schultz. My life is an open book. Everyone knows my lovely wife and our five girls. While my kids have taken me through a lot of challenges over the last couple of months, they're teenagers. Ask anybody raising young people, and they'll tell you the teen years are tough. I hope the good people of Charlotte, North Carolina, elect me to serve as their mayor. Not because I'm perfect, but because I want to make this city perfect for them," my dad eloquently said. I was proud of that powerful answer.

"So you're saying you're not perfect and you've got something to hide?"

"No, I'm not saying that at all."

"So there are no skeletons in your closet?"

"I don't know what you're getting at, Mr. Schultz," my dad said forcefully.

"Oh, well let him get to it!" Mr. Brown, the Republican candidate running against my father, said. "Everybody looks at me, digging all into my issues. Nobody in this city is perfect. You heard it from Sharp himself, so all of you guys who think he's the good one, the least of three evils, some folks are saying—"

"You don't live in my skin, and you don't live in my house, Brown," my father angrily cut him off.

A whole lot of oohs and aahs rang out from the crowd. My dad tugged on his suit jacket. I could tell he was trying to compose himself.

"I know you're not as meek and mild as everybody thinks you are, or I wouldn't have been able to trip you up just a second ago. So if anybody knows anything about Mr. Sharp, you might want to get it out there sooner rather than later before the people of Charlotte are blindsided." Mr. Brown verbally punched back, trying to jab my dad and take him down.

"And as you can see," the independent candidate burst in, "I don't deal with back-and-forth banter, nor am I affiliated with any party that is only for their own agenda. As your independent candidate, choose me so I can truly make sure the great citizens of this city are fully represented."

They took closing remarks from Mr. Brown and my dad, but I could tell both men were still hot under the collar. Mr. Schultz appeared pretty proud of himself, judging by the smirk on his face. He stood up after it was over and talked to the lady who gave me the water, and I waited for my dad to come off the stage so I could congratulate him.

While I was waiting, I overheard Mr. Schultz saying, "Yeah, he's got something to hide. This story has got legs. Look over there."

And when his head nodded toward the left—stage right—I saw my dad with a lady wearing a tight, red dress, fixing his blue tie. She was smiling. What didn't I know?

***

The girl standing with my father couldn't be older than thirty. She had on the latest styles. Her hair was flawless, and her stilettos were kicking. I had to figure out who this chick was fixing my dad's tie and smiling all in his face. She was way too close for comfort, and the rumors were already circulating.

Had my mom, sisters, and I been that naive? Did my dad have a whole other life going on? Maybe this lady was his baby momma. Oh, I had to quit dreaming up the drama, but I certainly needed to put a stop to all the coziness I was witnessing before my speculations came true. Just before I got over to them, they gave each other a hug, and she was gone.

I couldn't ask who she was because my mom came from a different direction. My dad kissed her on the lips and grasped her hand like all was good with the world. I just didn't appreciate him playing with my mom like that. She deserved way more. She deserved for me to tell her what I read, heard, and saw with my own eyes. But I wasn't an idiot. Some people were hating on my father. He was days away from possibly running this big, powerful city. What if he couldn't even see that this lady he was all chummy with was setting him up for failure? Would this be the beginning of his demise? I needed more details before I formed a final opinion.

***

I just kept tossing and turning in my bed. I couldn't sleep. My sisters invited me to watch a scary movie with them, but I didn't like movies that made the hair on my back stand straight up. My parents had retired for the evening. The thought of my dad's hands all over my mom after they had been on another woman irritated me to no end. I thought that if I got a little something to eat and listened to some cool music, then maybe that would change my mood.

When I came down the stairs, the first room I passed was my father's office. I stopped because I heard his cell phone going off. Without hesitation, I grabbed it, and it said Miss X.

There were four missed calls and then a text that read, "Where are you? Important!"

It was after ten o'clock. Where my dad was is not her business. Besides, what did she need to talk to him about that was so important? I wanted to scream, shout, and snatch my dad out of my parent's room to get to the bottom of this. But I just didn't want to hurt my mom, so I had to figure out another plan.

I paced back and forth in my dad's office. I wanted to text her back and say, "Don't ever call me again."

I didn't do it. I realized my dad would be able to see the text, and that would cause a bigger problem. Nothing could be done on cell phones these days that couldn't be traced. He didn't have a lock on his phone, but he would be able to see the time the text was sent and know that he didn't send it. I didn't want to piss him off. I wanted to protect him. I wanted to protect what he was building for us. While my sisters thought it was a big burden to be the first daughters of the city, I was enamored with the idea. As I thought of them, I realized maybe my sisters were the ticket. Maybe they could help me figure out the best way to undo what my father had done.

Without rethinking what I was about to do, I jetted down to the basement. The lights were off, and the TV was blaring. I went over to the tube and turned off the TV.

"We thought you were coming to watch the movie with us! Just 'cause you don't wanna see nothin' scary don't mean you need to be turning it off for the rest of us!" Shelby yelled, using all types of bad grammar.

"Yeah, if you need to turn it down, then turn it down," Ansli said, as she gave me a mean stare. "Don't turn it off."

"Did Mom and Daddy tell you to?" Yuri asked.

I shook my head. I prided myself in always telling the truth. Slade was asleep on the lounger, slobbering to the left side. I kicked her.

"Huh, huh! What part I miss? What part I miss?" Slade said, as Shelby motioned for her to wipe her face.

"You didn't miss anything," Ansli said.

Shelby grunted, "Yeah, dum-dum, she turned the movie off."

As Slade frowned, I frowned back and said, "I need to talk to you guys. This is important. We've got a real problem."

"You woke me up, so it better be a problem," Slade said.

"Y'all, seriously . . . I'm really, really worried."

"About what?" Shelby asked, irritated.

"Yeah, just spit it out, Sis. We were in the middle of a really good part," Ansli said in a sweeter tone, but she was still pushy.

"It's Dad."

"What's wrong with Dad?" Yuri questioned. I exhaled, happy that someone else was finally concerned.

I uttered, "I've got good reason to believe he's having an affair."

"Girl, you've got jokes," Slade said, as she took the pillow from behind her and flung it to my head.

I had good reflexes, so I caught the thing. "Watch it."

"Well, somebody's got to knock some sense into you," Shelby replied, cosigning on Slade's action.

"That does sound crazy," Yuri admitted, surprising me. She had always been on my side.

"Yeah, everybody knows Dad is smitten for Mom," Ansli added.

Yuri nodded. She got up and came over and gave me a hug. Then the youngest of the Sharp sisters, who was trying to act like my bestie, patted me on the head. Insulted, I moved away. I didn't need them to dismiss this. I needed them to understand the seriousness of all this. Obviously, I needed more proof. So I huffed and puffed, climbed the stairs, and left their tails alone.

"We love you though!" Ansli yelled.

"Yeah, even though you ain't turned back on the TV," Shelby shouted.

I loved them too, but sometimes they made me so mad. If they wanted proof, I was determined to find it. I didn't want this to be true. However, deep down I knew it was. I had a problem.

***

Going back to school on a Monday after a long weekend was actually refreshing for me. I was the studious one in the family. Though we all were smart, I loved academia.

I also loved the fall. Finally, it was getting chilly and I was able to bust out my new winter coat my mom had bought me at the end of last year when they were on sale. Though we had some dough, my parents were practical. The coat was cute. I wasn't into fashion like Shelby, but I did love to look adorable. Smart girls could rock it too. While I was walking in the hallway, I had to bump right into Reese Redman, the sophomore class Student Government Association president, who had been giving me grief all year.

"What's up, Sharp? Coming up in here all snazzy with your nose all up in the air?" Reese said as I kept walking. "What, you too cute to speak?"

"If I ain't say nothing, then there's your answer," I said as I walked right past him.

Gosh he got under my skin. Everything with the dude was always a coarse, joking statement. I so wanted him to leave me alone.

"Look here, we're signing up people today for PTSA. You need to join. I know your daddy sent you to school with loot. Give us a ten-spot."

The chump started grabbing at my purse. I had to snatch it away, and I wanted to smack his butt with it.

I said, "I don't want to join PTSA! I'm in my own clubs and activities."

Throwing his hands in the air, he tried a different approach. "Oh wait, so your daddy is about to be mayor, and you're too good to serve in our organization? Even if your status can help us?"

I put my hands on my hips. "Oh, you're admitting that who I am can help your cause? So you're saying you want to use me?"

Winking he said, "Basically!"

"Basically?" I questioned, frustrated he was even standing there saying this to me.

I just rolled my eyes. He stood there. The guy looked so serious, it was eerie, but why would I help him?

Finally feeling my angst, Reese said, "So that's a no? Final answer?" I figured if I just kept walking, he would understand that was my final answer, but then he followed me and got in my face.

"You could at least give me the respect to answer me."

"And when I give you the answer you don't want, that's not going to be enough for you."

Gently touching me, he said, "So then give me the answer I want."

"Urgh, the answer is NO," I vented, really exasperated with the jerk.

"Then go on with your highfalutin self," he said loudly to make me look bad. When other people in the hallway laughed, he knew he succeeded.

I wasn't used to people staring my way. Surely not for anything bad either. Reese called me out, and I didn't like that.

It was easy to forget the dum-dum because I was headed to my favorite class. Not even smart-aleck Reese Redmond—who was cute but for sure crazy—could stop me from being excited about journalism. Ms. Spears was a phenomenal teacher, and she loved my writing. Although I was a sophomore, she was positioning me to be the editor in chief of our new *Marks Magazine*. It was really a newspaper, but we wanted to call it something with an *M* to go with *Marks* to make it cooler. She was giving out assignments on who was going to write what for the second issue. I went over to her desk.

"I'm turning in the story on the debate. You are going to love it. The next issue, I want to be on the front page. Can you give me the top story?"

"Reserve the drama for the writing, Sloan. You know I wait to see all of the articles coming in. After I read them, I'll determine what should be on the front page . . ."

"Ms. Spears, come on now. You know who you want to write for the front page," I practically pleaded as I nudged her.

"And besides, Sloan, it needs to be a senior."

I leaned in closer. "Now you know none of the seniors can write like me. You said so yourself. Help me out. Give me the top story, and if you don't like what I write, then you don't have to keep me on the front."

"Okay, okay. There's a new student organization that's growing quickly." Ms. Spears handed me a paper.

I looked at the paper, and my eyes widened in shock at the subject matter. "What? Why do I need to write on a social club around here that has a lot of new members?"

"You want the cover story. The student part of the Parent Teacher Student Association is growing by leaps and bounds. We have more students signed up than parents or teachers. They have a meeting this afternoon. Go and see what you can find," she encouraged as she nudged me away.

At that moment, I got nauseous and felt like I had made a grave mistake. No way did I want to eat my words. I told Reese I wasn't interested. But I couldn't give up the top story. Actually, I was intrigued to see what he was doing to make people sign up. If I thought back, there was a line of people around a table he walked away from before he started walking with me. While his pitch to me was pathetic, maybe there was more than meets the eye. So I accepted the challenge.

The day couldn't go by fast enough. I was excited when school was over so I could go to room 212. That was where the students who were already in PTSA were meeting with interested students to talk about what the organization was supposed to do. I was familiar with PTSA. All of my life my mom had been a part of it, but I wasn't expecting the room to be packed with students. I didn't expect for Reese to be up at the front giving a moving speech like he was Dr. Martin Luther King Jr. himself.

"I have a dream. That teens in high school will come every day ready to seize their own education. You can walk into a building that is a new facility with the best equipment and best teachers, but if you aren't ready to take charge and make the most of the experience, then you're losing. You are needed to make Marks High School great. We're the future. We will craft the world, and this school can help us be all we're going to be. But we can't just take, we're supposed to give. Some of us have more to give than others," he said. I swore he looked directly at me.

"If we, the students, do more than our share, we can make sure that our parents and our teachers give us all that we need. And sometimes they won't know what we need until we tell them. The world is changing, technology is changing, and we've got to be on the cusp. You can be a football player or be an athlete in any sport and just do sports well, or you can be studious and make sure you take care of your lessons. But that's why I love PTSA, because whether it's sports, whether it's academics, whether it's social life, if it's happening in the halls of Marks High School, it affects us all. This organization can help the leaders make sure we stay Mavericks. Not just as a mascot, but in reality. Who's with me?" he said as he raised his arms.

Everyone cheered. Hands went up of students who wanted to sign up to be a part of his movement. I was impressed as the room lit up with spirit.

CHAPTER TWO
SHACKLES

"So are you going to join PTSA or what?" Reese said to me the next morning when I walked into the school.

I was actually planning to join. Even though I didn't want to admit it to myself, as hard as I tried to get his speech out of my head, I was bound to it. His words drew me in to his purpose. Willingly, I wanted to be a part of it. I just didn't like him asking me as if I couldn't resist his yucky charm or something.

"Yeah, we're both joining," my sister Yuri said as she took the form from the table and handed me another one to fill out.

Yuri knew me so well. As Reese came closer to me, my heart started beating faster and I became unresponsive. Yuri understood that the cat had my tongue. I appreciated her for speaking up for me.

She leaned over and said, "Now I see why you're making me do this. He wants you."

I jabbed her in the arm. Reese was obnoxious. I needed Yuri to pull me away from him, not push me to him. Shelby, Ansli, and Slade might have been bitten by love bug, but that was not on my radar at all. I had a rigorous class schedule. Except for journalism, French III, and PE, which I hated, I had all AP classes. I needed to get a 4.0 in my core classes. I didn't have time to get caught up with an intolerable guy like Reese Redmond, who always wanted things his way.

When I finished filling out the form, I handed it to Reese. The way his hand touched mine made me lose my breath. As our eyes locked on each other, I knew he was getting under my skin.

"Reese, who is this taking up all of your attention?" a cute girl sashayed over and interrupted.

"Okay, well I'll let you get back to your work," I said, seeing the girl roll her eyes at me.

But before I could walk away, Reese tugged on my hand. "Trevy, I want you to meet Sloan. Sloan, this is Trevy."

"We have gym together, but she doesn't notice me," Trevy said in a snide way.

Shaking my head, I responded, "No, I don't think we have a class together."

"Yes, you do. She's in your gym class," Yuri said in a breezy tone.

Feeling bad, I mouthed, "Sorry" at Trevy. I probably didn't know her because the girl seemed like a jerk who wasn't worth getting to know, not because I thought I was all that.

I always hated that on even-numbered days gym was my first class in the morning. You wake up and get all cute, and then you go to your first class and sweat. So to go to the next class, you have to take a shower to get all cute again. I liked when I had gym in previous years at the end of the day when I was already tired. Then once class was over, I didn't have to worry about taking a shower at school. I could go home and take a shower there. Some girls don't get clean after gym, but who wants to walk around school smelling bad all day? Not Sloan Sharp.

Once Reese introduced us, Trevy wasn't really trying to talk to me. Yuri was pulling on me so we could get to class. To keep it moving, I waved bye to Reese. He quickly waved bye back at me. That was that. Ending things was, for sure, the best; before anything could flare up, it was put out.

"That girl likes him," Yuri said to me.

"And? Why are you telling me?" I said to my sister as I rolled my eyes.

Tugging on my coat and stopping me from moving, Yuri replied, "Because it looks like she's not the only one."

"Whatever," I uttered as I flicked my hand, dismissing her nonsense theory that held no merit.

Not buying what I was selling her, Yuri joked, "Don't whatever me. I saw you looking at him like he's a spoon."

"Huh?"

"You hear me . . . looking at him like a spoon you were ready to lick."

Huffing in denial, I said, "You're imagining things."

"Why do you think he had to take your money and your paper from your hands? You were so goo-goo eyed you couldn't even tell you looked sprung. You're falling for him. I'm going to be the only Sharp sister alone."

"Nope, it's me and you, girl. Forget these boys. And a boy like that would want me jumping up and down for him. 'Stand on one leg, Sloan. Bark like a dog, Sloan.'"

The two of us laughed as we entered the locker room to change. There were actually three gym classes going on at one time, so while Yuri and I had the same class period, we had different teachers. And all of a sudden, the Trevy chick burst into the locker room and around to our side. She opened up a locker between Yuri's and mine.

"Hey, girls!"

"Hey," Yuri said, half wanting to speak.

"See ya later, Sis," I pushed her away and said right before she was gone.

"That's your sister, really?" Trevy asked as her nose turned up. "I mean, cuz like, you're so pretty, she's so plain."

"Excuse me!" I said to her.

"I'm just joking! I thought y'all were like play sisters or whatever . . ."

I didn't really know this girl, and though anything anyone wanted to know about my family was out there for the world to find, if she didn't know the details, I wasn't trying to tell her. Besides, Yuri and I were tighter than blood sisters.

"Alright, well I'll see ya later," I said to her.

"No, no, no. Maybe we got off on the wrong foot. Reese told me he thought I was a little harsh on you earlier. He said I was cold and stuff. I can come across like that, but really I wanted to tell you how much I admire you. I'm not the only one. He thinks you're so pretty."

"He does?" I uttered in a surprised yet interested tone.

Trevy stepped back, unsure how to take my response. "Yeah, but I mean what does he know? Every day he's saying girls are pretty. Not that you aren't pretty or anything like that, but . . ."

"Naw, I get what you're saying," I replied, understanding now that Reese was trying to play me.

"He'll tell a girl whatever she wants to hear."

"I see where you're going."

"Exactly!" Trevy said as her unsure face regained confidence. "We could be great friends. You're not fooled by the bull. Personally, I hate those girls who fall for any lines, thinking that the guy is only after them when he holds their hand an extra minute too long. But I wonder why he was talking about your teeth?"

My eyes squinted. "What do you mean about my teeth? I just got my braces off."

"Yeah, he said it seemed like it because you had some spots that were like yellow and some that were really white. I don't know. What does he know?" Trevy said, and her comment got under my skin.

I started walking to the court, and I was so mad. We were playing volleyball, and when it was my turn to serve, I wanted to kill whoever was on the other side of the net. The coach liked my enthusiasm, but afterwards I was even more bummed that I had worked up a sweat letting guy pressure stress me so much.

Adding insult to injury, when I went into my second class, there was Reese. How come I didn't notice all these people were in my classes before? When he spoke to me, I gave him the cold shoulder. Thankfully we didn't sit anywhere near each other in class, but when our teacher, Mr. Bonner, gave us a test and started walking around and telling people to change their answers, I looked up and looked right at Reese, who appeared equally annoyed.

Trying to be cool, Mr. Bonner said, "Don't trip. Some of y'all ain't studied, and my job is on the line about this AP class. So if I'm helping y'all a little bit too much, and you don't say nothing, we all will be okay."

But how could we all be okay? Some students were cheating, and others were honestly studying to earn a great grade. It wasn't right. Reese and I shook our heads hard and started back on our own work. I could tell he didn't think it was right either. Something was going to have to be done. But what?

***

"After you," Reese said to me as he nearly ran me over walking out of AP World History.

When I went to go left, he went left too. When I turned down the hallway on the right, he turned right too. He was on my heels.

"Are you following me?" I turned around and asked him.

"No, we got the same math class. You're cute and all, but nobody has time to be putting up with Miss High Maintenance," he said to me with a bit of an attitude.

I grunted and huffed thinking, "How dare he refer to me that way?" I couldn't let him get under my skin. I wondered why I hadn't realized we had a couple of classes together. Where had I been? Or maybe I did remember, it was just he wasn't standing out to me until now. I do recall a loud-mouthed jerk, but I never looked up to see who it was. Maybe it was him.

If I was honest, now I understood some of his words held meaning. Maybe he wasn't trying to bait me, but when he looked at me and winked, I thought he was flirting. Both of us were all over the place with each other—as far as emotions go, that is. Neither one of us wanted to show our hand, and after what Trevy told me he had been saying about me, maybe I was making a possible connection up all in my mind. Could he have an attraction to me?

Reese rubbed my shoulders and whispered, "Maybe you need a massage. Let me help you calm down a little bit."

The touch was for sure relaxing, but I didn't know how to take it. Where was he coming from? What did he expect me to say to this gesture? I moved away from his grip.

"I need to calm down too. I don't mean to come across so rude," he said, as he started walking with me instead of behind me. I didn't even tell him that was okay. "This school's got some issues. Like right now. We're going to math class, it is November, and we still don't have textbooks."

"You are so right," I said to him, irritated at the thought.

"It's math! How do they expect us to learn without textbooks?" Reese said. "See, Sloan, I'm not a member of PTSA just because I want to beef up my resume so it looks impressive for colleges. There are plenty of clubs I could get in for that. I really do want to make a difference. I also think it's ridiculous that in AP World History, Mr. Bonner is helping people cheat."

Smiling from ear to ear because he was right on, I said, "For real. I thought you were feeling that was wrong too."

"Cool, we both are disgusted. But the question is what are we going to do about it? And why is it alright for students to want that help? We've got to demand our own education."

"Alright, well, let's ask the teacher where our books are," I said to him. He was a gentleman and let me step into math class first.

He scoffed, "Good luck with that."

I headed right over to Ms. Peters and asked,

"Ms. Peters, do we have our books yet?"

"Nope, they're not in yet. So I need you guys to go ahead and copy down the new information from the board. Take about five minutes, and I'll be erasing it to give you more instructions. Then you'll have to copy the classwork problems off the board too, and we will go over the problems. Also, I've got a homework sheet you can pass around when you guys get in groups to copy it."

Hearing this ridiculous plan, Reese walked over to her desk and complained. "Ms. Peters, this just ain't right. Some copy slower than others. What if we write down the steps wrong and then it's erased? Who do we need to talk to about our books?"

Throwing up her hands, she said, "The principal, the school board, the superintendent, anybody but me. It's not like kids are rushing to carry that big heavy thing around anyway."

I interjected, "Yeah, but last class I copied down the instructions, and you erased it before I was even finished."

Reese said, "Right, a similar thing has

happened to me. I think I copied a step down wrong because when I went to work on the problem at home, it didn't make sense. I looked it up online, and there was a whole step missing."

Ms. Peters tried to reassure us. "I know these aren't advantageous circumstances for you guys to learn under, but I'm here before school, after school . . ."

"Yeah, yeah, yeah, we get that you are here for extra help, but that still does not change the fact. We should have some textbooks to take home too. Now we got to break into groups and copy down homework problems. This is crazy," Reese said.

Frustrated, I uttered, "And it's not right. Because what if he copies them slow or what if I copy a question wrong? You can't even go back and look at it because it is not in a textbook. Like, we can't get copies to put in our three-ring binders?"

Ms. Peters said, "No, because the county's got me short on supplies."

"This is bull," Reese said, getting more upset.

"Watch your mouth!" Ms. Peters told him.

I wanted to calm him down, but I was equally angry. Knowing there was nothing more we could do, we went to our seats. We got through class doing what we were told.

As soon as it was over, he was waiting for me and asked, "You headed to lunch?"

"Yeah," I told him as we walked to the cafeteria together.

"So what we gonna do? You joined PTSA. You gonna help me change this thing? Your dad being the mayor and all, I know he can help us draw attention to this foolishness. This ain't right. Taxpayers pay money to help the kids. Not for the money to go into peoples' pockets. If we don't have textbooks and we don't have paper, somebody's stealing. I'm just saying," Reese shared.

I put my hand on his shoulder, and he looked over at me. We stopped walking at that moment and shared a strong look. I didn't want him to get so upset, so frustrated, and so discouraged. I needed him to be calm, still passionate, but respectful so that we could figure out a plan and get things done. We did not need our attitudes to be perceived the wrong way so that we would get shut down before we got to stand up.

"Excuse me, are you two going to lunch, or you just going to stand in the hallway?" Trevy came between the two of us and said.

"Oh, dang," Reese said. "I left the history book in math class. I'll catch up."

"Gotcha," I said as he jetted back. Then I looked at the girl standing real close. "I'll see you later, Trevy."

She tugged me back. "No, don't go. Let's walk together."

"Why?" I looked at her and said.

"I just want to tell you how petty Reese is. I don't know what y'all are all chummy talking about, but obviously you didn't get what I was saying before."

Unsure of her motives, I said, "No, I heard you. He was talking about me."

"Yeah, and not just your teeth. He called you an airheaded, stuck-up wench. He said he had no problem using you so that he could get what he wants. I guess he knew what he was talking about," Trevy said before she walked on ahead.

Moments later, Reese caught up with me. "Glad you're still here. You ready to go?"

"Not ready to go anywhere with you," I said, as I stormed off, mad at his audacity.

Before I could get too far, Ms. Spears stopped me and pulled me into an empty classroom. "I read the first draft of your article on the growth of PTSA, Sloan, and honestly, I'm disappointed. No way it is publishable material."

Confused, I said, "Why? What's wrong with it?"

"You need to look at it again. Please don't submit first drafts that are this grammatically incorrect in the future. In addition, though, you've got to dig deeper into the story. You're going to have to talk to your subject, get to know him, not just breeze over information. Make it juicy so people want to read it. I know this isn't what you expected to hear because most of your work I've loved, but unfortunately, I don't love this one."

She turned around and left me there. It was hard to hear I wasn't as great a writer as I thought. I had no problem working hard, but now I was going to have to work hard with Reese. A guy I was going to have to be tied to even though I wanted to get far away from him. I was falling for his baloney. No more. Even if I had to talk to him to get the information I needed, I wasn't going to let him affect me. I was cutting the emotional ties.

***

School had been so crazy that I had forgotten that this was my father's big day. We would find out in a matter of hours whether or not my dad was going to be the next mayor of the city of Charlotte. Thinking about it, I was excited, yet nervous.

"Come on. Our sisters are already gone," Slade said to me.

It was so weird. I was usually on top of everything. But I was off my game. Reese was invading my skin like the plague, but for some reason, I didn't want an antidote, and that was really bothering me. I knew he was a jerk. Trevy had confirmed that. Why couldn't I shake him?

"What's going on with you?" Slade probed as we got into the car.

"I can't explain it." She was my wild sister—not the one I'd ask to help me think straight.

"It's a guy, isn't it?"

Shocked by how accurate she was, I said, "Have you been talking to Yuri?"

"No, but it *is* a guy? Who is it? Oh, I knew your cute little self couldn't stay single for long."

"It is not a guy."

"Um hm," she moaned in a singsongy tone, not believing me.

"No, seriously, Slade," I said as my sister gave me a look that told me she wanted the scoop. "Alright, if it was a guy, I mean let's just say *if* it was . . ."

"Yeah, yeah, yeah, I'm with you. If it was, then what?"

"How do you know if he likes you too? It could be hard to tell if he is arrogant and rude, and if somebody tells you he's talking about you."

"Well, if the guy is talking about you and it gets back to you . . . he likes you."

"What if what I'm told he's saying isn't flattering?"

"The person isn't telling the truth?"

"Does it matter? If he says something that's not nice, then should I believe that he likes me under any circumstances? I mean who says that because somebody talks about you, that that means they like you?"

"Well, I can see you are all wrapped up in this."

"Where we going?" I asked, when she passed the exit to our house.

"To a hotel."

"I don't understand."

"We're staying at the hotel tonight where dad's gonna accept the mayoral win or give some kind of concession speech. Mom's got our outfits there."

"He won't have to concede," I said to my sister.

"I'm just saying, either way it goes, we've got to smile. But get back to this guy. Obviously, he goes to Marks." I nodded. "That's a good thing because with my boo at a different school,

41

I never get to see him."

"Yeah, but y'all's first encounter you said Avery came up to you and basically told you not to cry, called you beautiful, and the rest is history. My start with this guy has been all rocky."

"Knew it was a guy," Slade said as he smiled. "He's under your skin."

"I was just thinking that I can't shake this dude," I told her.

"So don't fight it."

"But his best buddy . . ."

"Oh, he probably likes you."

"No, his best buddy is a girl."

"Oh! Well, she's lying. Whatever she's telling you, I wouldn't even believe that."

"What do you mean she's lying? You don't even know what she said."

"If she's coming to you telling you a whole bunch of stuff after you and him have a moment, then that's because her tail wants to be with him. Don't fall for it."

"No, it's nothing like that."

"So why are you so confused by what she says and how he's reacting? There's something to it. I'm telling you. Or maybe she wants you herself."

"Maybe because I am that fine," I joked back.

"Just be open, Sloan. If there is anything there, it will do what it do."

My sister had been in the music world far too long. Those loud bass beats were getting to her head. For real though, I got where she was coming from. Actually, she gave me the words I needed to hear.

Three hours later, the Sharp sisters looked sassy. My mom looked nervous. My dad looked confident. Though we were in a suite, outside our family's door was a whole bunch of pomp and circumstance of press and people who were a part of my dad's campaign. We were all waiting on the final results. Only 32 percent of the precincts had reported, but my dad was already ahead.

I went over to him and said, "You're going to win this thing. You've got this."

Hugging me tight, he said "That's right my lil' sweetheart."

"Don't get all cocky over there," my mom said to us.

"You've got to believe," he said back to her. Then he looked at me and my sisters. "And even if this isn't for me, girls, we fought a hard, clean campaign while things tried to get messy around us. We did a lot for the city already, and I can concede with my head held high. Truth is, when you look within and you know you've done all you can do, if it don't work out, it ain't for you. And that's not always a bad thing."

I nodded, appreciating hearing that. It seemed like the next two hours took forever to go by. When was the night going to be over?

Finally, my father's campaign manager burst into our room and said, "You got to come on out! All stations are declaring you the winner! Brown and James have conceded."

Our hotel suite erupted as my dad looked at all of us, took my mom's hand, and said, "I've got a beautiful family. Just how we ran this race is how we're going to run this city. I might get busy, girls, but your dad is always here. I love you guys."

I was proud of him. I felt like we were city royalty, and he wasn't even sworn in yet. What a tremendous feat he accomplished. My parents led the way out the door, and we followed them. Then everybody in my dad's campaign followed us down the hallway, down the steps, and finally we got to the gorgeous foyer five stories below. As soon as we stepped out, more cheers rang out.

Before my dad was about to take the podium, I saw that same mysterious lady, Miss X, trying to get to him. I was so happy when my mom and others wouldn't let my dad stop walking up the stairs. I saw the way she was looking at him, like she was mad she couldn't talk to him. When I tried to go talk to her and find out what the heck was going on, one of my sisters tugged me away. When I looked back, she was gone.

We immediately went onstage and stood behind my dad. He couldn't even give his speech because the cheers and applause just wouldn't stop coming. My dad had done it! He had achieved his dream. He was going to be the mayor of Charlotte. All the ugliness of politics and campaigning was behind him. We were done with that. Gone were the shackles.

CHAPTER THREE
SPECULATE

"Well, sorry I couldn't get here before your mayor-elect got up and gave a speech, but I guess he just couldn't wait for me to concede," said Mr. Brown, surprising us all by coming onstage and taking the mic.

No one laughed, though Mr. Brown was trying to make a joke. I could only imagine how he felt. It couldn't be easy to lose an election, to put your whole heart into it, and to have it not turn out the way you want. However, Mr. Brown had proven to be a despicable man, and the citizens of Charlotte showed him by electing my father by a landslide.

"Okay, okay, I see you guys didn't get the joke. Well, really, I want to congratulate Mr. Sharp and his family. Shucks, maybe I need to go get a bunch of beautiful girls, and I could win next time." Again, no one laughed. "In all seriousness, we're going to have a fine mayor. And Mr. Sharp, I wanted to let you know I am here to serve you however you need. It's all about the city of Charlotte, right?" Finally, he got a bunch of cheers. "Let's keep it Sharp!"

My dad nodded to thank everyone, and the crowd erupted. Mr. Brown went over to my father, grabbed his hand, and lifted both of their hands in the air. Mr. Brown was pointing at my dad and bowing in front of him, like he was a king or something. My father looked uncomfortable, but he graciously played along.

"That man is full of crap," Shelby said, standing by me.

She knew best. After all, it was her boyfriend's mother who was married to the jerk. I couldn't believe the lady admitted at a public event that her husband was abusing her. I didn't know much about where their relationship had gone, but she did move out. Ever since that happened, the public pulled away from him.

My dad's campaign manager took the mic and said, "Alright . . . enough of the speeches, let's celebrate the victory because, thanks to you all, we did it!"

"Thanks, Brown, for coming," I heard my dad say to Mr. Brown as he tried to take his hand back.

Mr. Brown wouldn't let it go though. "You could have waited for me to get here to say some words before you accepted. That's real tacky."

My father retorted, "I thought you conceded in your own hotel. I didn't know you were coming over here to congratulate me too. You didn't give any of my staff a heads-up."

Frowning and cocking his head, Mr. Brown uttered, "So . . ."

"So either you meant you are going to support me, or you are planning to continue the foe mentality," the mayor-elect stated.

Mr. Brown stomped and said, "Whatever. You're going to run this city into the ground."

Fed up, my dad said, "Alright, that's enough. You don't have to speak with all this hostility in front of my family."

"Your family? Like you care about them . . ."

"Watch your mouth," my dad said to him.

"Stanley, come on, honey," my mom said to my father as she placed her delicate arm in his. "Obviously, he's dealing with the loss. Let's leave him to it."

He kissed my mom lightly on the cheek, and they walked off the stage. My four sisters followed, Shelby rolling her eyes harder than I'd ever seen her do. Actually, she looked like she wanted to punch the man.

Shelby wasn't the only one who was angry. I wanted to tell him off too. Yeah, he was my elder, but he was acting like a baby. He didn't need to ruin this night for my father. When he walked off the stage, I followed him. After all, investigation was in my blood. Was he spouting lies, or was there some truth to what he was mouthing off about?

"Mr. Brown, Mr. Brown!"

"What!" he rudely screamed before turning

around and seeing it was one of the Sharp girls. "Oh . . . you," he said, smiling like we were old friends.

"What you just said to me, my family . . . why would you say that?" I asked in a cold tone.

Even colder, he said, "Because I meant it. Your dad is a pretender. Everybody thinks his stuff is all in order, like his hands aren't dirty. He gets my life exposed while he stays clean . . . I've done my investigating, and clean he is not."

"Sir, I don't believe you," I said, even though deep down I did have doubts.

He reached into his coat jacket. I was afraid to see what he was searching for. He pulled out a picture, but I could only see the back.

He turned it toward me and said, "I'm not trying to ruin your world, even though mine got ruined tonight. But what's this?"

My eyes bucked wide. "It's my dad."

"Right, and that ain't your momma. They're mighty close, and this was taken in the window of a hotel. Your sweet lil' dad close to a girl who looks closer to your age than his age," Mr. Brown stated with too much enthusiasm.

I knew who the lady was. That was clearly Miss X. She and my father at a hotel? Mr. Brown was right. My family was falling apart, and most of the people in the Sharp family had no clue. Now that I knew, I was determined to make sure our demise didn't happen.

"That's my gift to you, sweetie. You enjoy that cozy photo," Mr. Brown stated as he patted my head and strolled out of the ballroom.

I couldn't show it to my sisters right away. I had to come up with a plan. I was going to save my family. No doubt about it.

***

"Okay, so I know, Ms. Spears, you were really excited about me rewriting the article about why PTSA is growing. I got that, and I'm on it. I promise I am going to work on it. Now, I have got a whole other idea that I think is even bigger to go on the front page. You're going to love this. Seriously, seriously, you're going to love this!" I said.

"Alright, settle down, Sloan. I love the passion, but you also have to be able to present.

When you're too fired up, sometimes the idea doesn't come across. Take a deep breath, slow down, and tell me what you're talking about. What's this juicy story?" my journalism teacher said.

"I want to write about how the teachers at Marks High aren't really for us."

Shaking her head, making an ugly face, like I'd offended her, she said, "You want to do what?"

I calmly responded, "Okay, not all the teachers, but I want to write it about how there are some shady teachers here at Marks High. I want to expose them. I want to break the story."

The expression of sheer disgust on her face became more intense. However, I wasn't going to back down.

I pressed, "I can give you the details. I'm not going to make anything up. If I put it in print, it's going to be factual."

"Sloan, you know how hard it was for us to get the administration to let us start this paper. It had to be okayed by the principal, who had to get it approved by the superintendent, and the superintendent had to let the board approve it. There are only certain types of content we are allowed to put in here. Bashing the school system is not one that is allowed."

"I'm not trying to bash the school system. I'm just going to call out a few shady teachers or things that are going on that aren't working in the best interest of the students. That's what we're supposed to be reporting: real news, right? This isn't just some fluff magazine."

"I've already given you a story. Why don't you work on getting that corrected before you jump on to something else?"

"So are you saying you don't want my story?"

"I'm saying you're not the editor. Write what you're given, and do that well."

"Well, maybe I should be the editor, to push the envelope, to get to the readers who want true news," I replied.

Ms. Spears stepped closer to me and said, "I know you're feeling yourself because your dad was just elected mayor."

Cocking my head back at her comment, I explained, "That's not true. I'm not trying to cross you, but at the same time, I'm not going to let you bring down my dreams either."

"Trust me on this . . . let it go."

"Okay, fine. Can I go interview this SGA guy?"

"Now that's what I'm talking about," Ms. Spears said in a nicer tone. "You sure can, but only if he is in a class that he can be pulled out of."

"It should be no problem because he's in weight training. I've done my due diligence. He already has permission to talk to me for fifteen minutes."

"Okay, then I'll expect you back before the class period ends."

"The nerve of her," I said to myself when I stepped into the hallway.

"The nerve of who?" Reese came up behind me and said, startling me.

"You scared me!" I said, hitting his hand.

"You looking for me, right?"

I nodded. "I was on my way to the gym."

"My teacher told me that I needed to come to your classroom."

"My classroom is the last place I want to be right now."

"Another teacher tripping, huh?"

"You don't know the half of it."

"Talk to me," he said as he playfully nudged me.

"We've got to figure out where I'm going to interview you," I said, trying to make the interaction professional.

We walked into the media center. There was a couch and a chair. We went over and sat down.

"Okay, talk to me," Reese said acting all concerned.

"You're not supposed to be interviewing me," I said to him, not wanting pity. "I'm supposed to be interviewing you."

"Talk to me, Sloan. What's got you so mad?"

"Like you care . . ." I said, not even knowing why I said it—probably trying to hide my feelings that I couldn't stop from growing.

"If I didn't care, I wouldn't have asked. I don't know what's up with you. Sometimes you're so warm and cool, and then other times you're so cold and hot under the collar. Am I doing something to you?" he asked.

"Today it's not you," I huffed and said being too honest. "Here I am on the newspaper. I want to be a reporter to tell the public the real deal. I want to inform people, give them breaking news they don't have so that they can use it for change. But when people in charge of the paper won't let me report stuff because it could hurt their job or something, it's like, why do politics have to be involved in everything? I know my dad just became the mayor, but I don't know, I feel like I've had enough politics to last me a lifetime. I'm tired of playing games."

"Well don't get frustrated with it. Until you're able to be a decision maker you walk within the guidelines you're given. But that doesn't mean you still don't write what you want to write. Even if it's just to get it out of you, even if it's just to put it on your computer, there'll be a time when you can use it. It's like me with my speeches. When I got something to say, sometimes it just comes from nowhere and I got to get a handheld voice recorder. I got to get it out when I got something to say. You should do the same thing; that's all I'm saying. Adults rule the world. But we don't have to be limited by their way of thinking."

I just wanted to reach out, grab Reese's neck, and hug him so tight. I so needed to hear that. Now I understood another reason why he was a motivational speaker. He wasn't just spouting rhetoric; deep down he was profound, and I liked that.

"So, what do you need to ask me about for the interview?"

"Honestly, I think I'm good. Just knowing what you said to me, every student in the school needs to know the same thing. Don't be limited, think outside the box, and settle for nothing less."

"Yeah, that's me. I said all that?" he joked.

"Maybe not in so many words" I teased back. "But you're alright, Reese."

"I think the same thing about you, Sloan Sharp," he said, as our hands found their way to touching.

"Urgh, excuse me!" my sister Yuri came over and said, startling me.

Yuri eyed Reese. We were sitting sort of close. He and I jumped far apart, like we had been caught kissing or something.

"Well, that's it, Reese. Thanks."

"That's why I popped in. I knew you really liked that boy!" my sister declared when the two of us were far from Reese.

"I do not."

"He's cute!" she admitted.

"He's sweet!" I responded.

"Yeah, if I had a million dollars, I'd bet y'all would become a couple because you like him."

"Don't waste money you can't make back. There's nothing to it," I said, blowing off my growing feelings for Reese.

"Okay, if that's what you want to tell yourself. But I see love in your future."

I just smiled. Reese was cool because during my journalism class, I was fuming, but he had turned all that around. Maybe there was something there.

***

My sisters and I hadn't had a chance to hang out

like normal teenagers in a long time. Last month we were able to go and get hamburgers together. So earlier in the week, we planned to hang out on Friday night and go to the big football game.

"As soon as we get in the game, these two . . ." I said as I pointed at Shelby and Ansli. ". . . gon' be with their boyfriends."

"Right, right," Slade laughed and said.

"Oh, you would be too if yours went to this school," I told her.

"This is sister time. I promise that's not gonna happen," Ansli said.

"That is until the second half," Shelby said as she hit Ansli in the side.

I gave them both a look. Shelby blew me a kiss. I knew she wanted to hang with her boo. I frowned because I really wanted to hang with them with no male interruptions.

Shelby threw her arm around me, "I'm just playing, girl! Go, Mavericks!"

As soon as we got to the gate, there was a table straight ahead that said Parent Teacher Student Association. I saw Reese standing with an older gentleman.

The handsome man who looked to be in his forties stepped toward me and my sisters. "Who in the world are these pretty ladies?"

"Dad!" Reese said, clearly embarrassed.

"What? I'm sure they get that all the time," Reese's father said.

I stepped behind my sisters. I guess I was embarrassed too. We did get comments that we were cute a lot. But I'd never gotten them from the father of a guy who intrigued me. Also, I didn't want my sisters to see I was frazzled.

Mr. Redmond said, "You ladies look familiar. I know you are not the Kardashians, but you could be."

Ansli and Yuri did look like them, but I knew Shelby was about to say, "Okay, Mr. Too-old-to-be-macking-to-the-high-school-girls . . . we'll see ya."

"Wait now, hold on. My son is SGA president. I just wondered had you guys joined PTSA."

"Yes, sir. I have," Yuri raised her hand and said. "Me and my sister."

Yuri tried to point me out. When she moved

to the left, I moved to the left. When she moved to the right, I moved to the right. Then she did a double take, and I thought she was turning left, but she really moved to the right, so I was exposed.

"And who is this?" Mr. Redmond said with a large grin.

Mumbling, I could make out that Reese replied, "Dad, that's Sloan."

"Sloan? Ohhhhh, Sloan. Well, why don't you ask her to work with you?" his dad said before looking at me and my sisters. "A couple people were supposed to be helping over here at the booth, but they didn't show. We won't keep you too long. I'm at another table on the visitors' side. I don't want Reese here standing all alone. A pretty girl like you might get us more memberships. You up for it?"

"Not tonight. I'm spending time with my sisters. We're just having girl time," I said, quickly declining.

"All you guys sisters? Wow!"

Shelby said to me: "Well, we want you to serve. We'll be right in the stands," Shelby patted me on the back, got close to my ear, and said, "Oh, isn't this ironic. Who's with a boy now? You've been holding out."

Before I could say no, my sisters were gone, leaving me there with Reese and his dad. His dad was gathering paperwork to take to the other table. I felt really awkward.

Mr. Redmond checked me out once more before jetting. "Thanks for staying here to work with my son. You said she was gorgeous, Reese, good eye."

"Dad!" Reese said, as his brown face turned red.

Then it was just the two of us. It was still very uncomfortable. I wasn't prepared, but I did look cute. Shelby made sure all of us looked good when we stepped out. I could see Reese focusing on my booty.

"So, um, you told your dad I was cute?" I teased.

He tried to deny it. He looked away. He looked up, but his flushed face told on him.

"Yeah, he asked me what was going on at school, and um, you are for sure going on."

Now Reese had me blushing. "So what are we doing here? What are you at the table for?"

"We're signing up memberships and taking donations."

"For what?"

"We feed the teachers once a month before school."

"Even the shady ones?" I said.

"You got a good point with that."

In a booth next to ours was the Mavericks Shop booth. It held all the paraphernalia. Our assistant principal, Mr. Hobby, who always seemed too busy to really talk, was manning it. His line was long. Since Marks was a new school, a lot of people didn't have sweatshirts, T-shirts, baseball caps, hoodies, and the like. Reese and I were looking right at him. We were both caught off guard when his line was gone and he didn't put the money for the last sale in the cashbox right in front of him. Instead, he stuck it in his pocket.

"Did you see what I just saw?" Reese asked me.

"Oh, my gosh, I did! He stole that money.

See what I'm saying. These adults are supposed to be here for us, and every time you turn around, we find more wrong than right. We got to go and see what's up with him."

Trevy walked up, blocking our view. When we stepped around her, it appeared Mr. Hobby was about to walk away.

"We've got to catch him," I said to Reese.

"Yeah, Trevy, we got to bounce. Watch the table. We need to go deal with the assistant principal. Something's not right," he told her.

"What you mean, something's not right?" Trevy asked.

"He's stealing," Reese let out.

"What? You go, Reese, let me talk to Sloan," Trevy insisted as she pushed him toward the apparel booth.

I tried to go after him, but Reese was gone, and there I stood.

"I just wanted to tell you thanks for being here with Reese. I was late. I'm so excited to see you working. You didn't just join PTSA, but you're standing with us. I know that means a lot to him, and it means a lot to me."

"Oh, okay."

"Can I borrow your phone?" she said. "I need to call my mom and let her know I made it here, and I left my phone at home."

Trying to spot Reese, I said, "Yeah, sure." I handed it to her.

"Can you unlock it? I don't want your code or anything, but . . ."

"Yeah, yeah, yeah," I uttered, annoyed. I unlocked the phone while still looking at Reese's back.

When I tried to hand it back to her, she said, "Oh, you know what . . . my phone's right here. Duh! I didn't think I would have left without it. Here ya go."

"Okay . . ." I said.

Trevy was acting weird. "So, you're not gonna hang here with me?"

"The game is about to start, and I'm going to go sit with my sisters after I catch up with Reese."

"Reese will be fine. The assistant principal isn't into anything. You guys definitely saw wrong, I'm sure."

I said, "But you weren't here. You don't know what we saw."

Rolling her eyes my way, Trevy said, "I'm just saying. It's not good to speculate."

CHAPTER FOUR
SACRIFICE

"Come on, Sloan," Reese came back over to the table and said to me. "I've been waiting on you. I think he's got the money in his left pocket. He's over there by the concession stand."

"I've been detained," I uttered, looking straight at his girl, who was standing in my way.

Reese squinted. "I don't understand."

"I didn't either at first, but I got it now. This one here is having a few issues with me and you talking."

"Urgh, how could you say that?" Trevy said.

Finally standing up to this girl, I said, "I'm

sick of playing games with you, Trevy. Something is going on between you and Reese."

Rolling her eyes, Trevy retorted, "No, something is going on between *you* and Reese."

"Yeah, but whatever, how can anything go on? Every time I think he's halfway cool, you tell me he's talking about me."

"You told her what?" Reese replied in dismay.

"Yeah, she told me you talked about my teeth stains, and you said I'm an airhead. She made it seem like there was much more you'd said. I was furious, but now I don't think you said any of that. She wanted me so pissed at you that we wouldn't even be talking now," I said happy the secret was out.

"Trevy, seriously? Tell me you didn't."

Trevy placed her hands on her hips. "What? You don't even really know this girl, and you did say she and her sisters think they're all that."

"No, I said her and her sisters *are* all that," Reese explained.

"No, you didn't," Trevy argued back.

"Yes, I did. And you were upset then that I was being friendly with Sloan. So it really doesn't surprise me now that you've been selling me out to her. I thought we were past all this," Reese said as he gave Trevy a mean glare.

Trevy went over and touched Reese's arm. "But I just can't get over it."

"Okay, past what? Over what? What am I missing?" I cut in and said as I crossed my arms feeling the chill in the night's air.

The two of them looked at each other like I was supposed to get it, like I knew. I'd had my head so far up a book for years that I was naive to a lot, especially relationship signs.

Seeing Trevy look into Reese's eyes, I said, "Oh . . . ooohhh. You two used to date. He was your man?"

Trevy rolled her eyes my way. "And you got a problem with it?"

Reese stepped up to Trevy. "Why you doing this? Why can't you let us go?"

"I just want another chance. That's all," Trevy uttered in a desperate tone.

Shaking my head, I sighed and said, "My sister was right! You do like him."

"Which sister?" They both looked at me

and said.

Irritated, I voiced, "Does it matter? You thinking I'm some kind of threat. There's nothing going on between us."

Reese grabbed my hand. "But it's not because I don't want there to be." He looked at Trevy. "And don't be lying saying we're together and stuff."

"I didn't say anything about us being together."

"Nope, she sure didn't. I didn't know anything." I said to him.

"Well, don't lie, saying I said negative stuff about her when the only thing I have said has been real positive. I want to get to know you more, Sloan. I'm sure a lot of guys are coming at you and your sisters. Y'all are beautiful girls."

"So what. Beautiful is overrated," Trevy yelled. "I'm so sick of people at school going nuts over the Sharp sisters.

"Don't hate," I looked at her and said, knowing she'd pushed me far beyond my comfort zone. I was *not* conceited.

A part of me wanted Reese just to spite her,

but that part was small. The bigger part of me wanted him because I could see in his eyes he really wanted me. The question in my mind was, is their thing done? Or was there more to the story that I didn't know?

"So what happened between the two of you guys?" I blurted out, breaking the silence.

"You want to tell her, or do I need to?" Reese said as he looked unhappily toward Trevy.

And from the way he said that, I figured out Ms. Trevy had been the one who had done something wrong.

When she was hesitant, I said, "What? You were too clingy? You stalked him? You gave it up too soon? What?"

"Naw, she gave it up to somebody else," Reese spit out, making my eyes open really wide.

I wasn't expecting for him to say that, and I don't think Trevy wanted him to tell me either. This girl had some nerve.

"Oh my gosh, you did? You hurt him, and now you don't want him to talk to anybody else."

All of a sudden, Mr. Hobby, the assistant principal came walking by, and instead of Trevy letting us deal with him directly, she turned and said, "Hey, excuse me, sir. We want to talk to you about stealing money."

"Huh, excuse me?" he said.

I wanted to pop her. I couldn't believe she just uttered that, spooking the man. Now he had his guard up.

Trevy smiled his way and said, "Yeah, these two right here think they saw you stealing."

"I don't know how they would have thought that," Mr. Hobby said, frowning at me and Reese.

When Mr. Hobby kept staring my way for an explanation, I said, "Yeah, we, um, were watching you from right here. Saw you put something in your left pocket."

He emptied his left pocket, stepped closer to me, and said, "Listen, I know your family is important, but you don't want to cross me."

"She's not the only one who saw you," Reese stepped in between us and said. "I did too."

Mr. Hobby shouted, "Well, you all are wrong! You don't need to go around accusing administrators, threatening our jobs for no reason."

"Well, you don't need to go around threatening students. My dad wouldn't take too kindly to the way you were just talking to me," I said, sick and tired of everybody thinking they could say whatever they wanted to me.

Teachers weren't just supposed to have these jobs for themselves. Even administrators were supposed to serve the students. Yes, I understood that it was a job. I knew that they had to pay their bills, but they didn't need to lie, steal, cheat, and threaten.

"You and your little girlfriend here need to back up. Got any other questions for me?" Mr. Hobby said, like we accused him wrongly.

Reese put his hands in the air and backed up. "Our bad."

"Exactly," Mr. Hobby said.

"But you owe her an apology on the way you just talked to her though. That wasn't cool," Reese demanded.

"If you thought I threatened you, miss, then my apologies." Then he leaned in closer to me and said, "But I meant what I said."

I started shaking. Mr. Hobby rolled his eyes and walked off. I was very frustrated that the whole encounter occurred in the first place.

"How you going to defend her? I really thought that we had a chance," Trevy yelled at Reese before he could check her.

"You gon' get with my cousin, and you think we have a chance?" he said, letting another bomb drop.

Shocked, I said, "It was his cousin?"

The more I knew about all the details between the two of them, the less I wished I knew. Trevy was trifling. Before the month started, love wasn't on my mind. Now I was open to it. It was clear to me that she didn't deserve a second chance. He was way too cool of a guy to settle for her crap. Why should I always be the one yielding? Sometimes it is just time to go for it.

Trevy placed her arm in Reese's. The chick was not backing off at all. When he didn't walk away, I turned to leave. He quickly stepped to me then and grabbed my arm.

"Please, let go of my arm," I said to Reese. I

wanted to go and sit with my sisters to watch the rest of the football game.

"Come on, Sloan, just let me talk to you for a second," he begged.

"What do you have to say to me?" I uttered.

Trevy was standing there practically breathing fire down his neck, looking at me like she wanted to throw daggers my way. And he wanted me to stand there and talk to him? As bad as I wanted them to be done, what they had was not through.

"Trevy, could you please give us some privacy?" Reese said, sensing I was uncomfortable.

With her watery eyes, she pleaded that he should give her a second chance. He shook his head in rejection. She threw up her hands and stomped away.

"Now it's just me and you," he said in a relaxing tone.

"Okay," I said, trying to sound uninterested. "What did you want to talk to me about?"

"Us . . ."

"Us?" I laughed. "There is no *us*."

"I sense there's something starting. Now

that you know all my relationship history, I want to lay all my cards out on the table. I like you, Sloan. I tried to come at you in a sly, slick sort of way, but you deserve to know what's up."

Trying to not get pulled into the mess, I said, "You're not finished with whatever you got going on with Trevy."

"Yes, we're done. You didn't hear what I said? I caught her cheating with my cousin. I'm not going down that route no more."

"Well, this road's blocked too."

"Why you doing that when you know you want to be with me?"

"That's mighty presumptuous, Reese."

"So I'm just making up this magnetic force between us? I can't take my eyes off you. I've been longing to do this," Reese said as he leaned in and kissed me.

I wanted to smack him. I wanted to pull him even closer. I didn't know what I wanted to do. So confused, I yanked away and ran off to find my sisters. Instead, I bumped right into our assistant principal, Mr. Hobby. "Listen, you know I wasn't stealing anything, right?"

I shrugged my shoulders. I didn't have any time for his bull, but he wouldn't move. Thinking back on what just happened, I wiped my mouth, still not believing I had been kissed for the very first time.

"I don't know, sir. If you say so, okay," I said, trying to step around him.

"No, you need to know I didn't because I don't want you going around telling people what you think you know and have that cause me a lot of drama. So, we settled it, right?"

"Okay." I said, willing to admit anything that would make him go away.

"Good, because I have a wife and kid. I don't have the next mayor in my back pocket. I've got to look out for me and make my own way. I had a baby at a young age. I had to put myself through school. So I was working two, three jobs."

I didn't need him to hate on me because he made bad choices. Again, I just tried to walk around him, but he stepped the same way I did. He would not let me get to the other side.

Once more, using a scary tone, he said, "If I

don't have this job, I don't have anything."

"Okay, sir," I uttered loudly as I stepped back.

Now I knew he had taken the money. He was going way overboard, trying to ensure that I didn't turn him in.

Since I had no proof, I firmly looked him in his eyes and said, "I'm not going to say anything right now."

He went off. "Right now? What, what does that mean?"

"Okay, I'm not going to say anything. Now, please move."

Our principal, Dr. Garner, came by and said, "Is everything okay over here?"

Mr. Hobby stepped out of the way and said, "Yeah, just congratulating Miss Sharp here on being one of the first daughters."

"Is that true?" Dr. Garner asked me.

That made me think he had some doubts on Mr. Hobby himself. Still, I nodded. No need in making things worse just yet.

"Have you seen my sisters, sir?" I asked, looking on the home side of the stands.

"Yes, they are sitting right up top of the

student section," Dr. Garner said, still sounding cautious of Mr. Hobby.

"Okay, thanks," I said before taking off.

Seeing Shelby, Ansli, Slade, and Yuri was sure a sight for sore eyes. I practically missed the whole game. Now it was going into the fourth quarter, but thankfully, Marks was winning.

"Tell us about the boyfriend!" Shelby said, striking up a conversation as soon as she saw me. The game was nothing much to watch.

"There's nothing to tell," I told the four of them in a strong tone. I didn't want any of them to ask me any questions, particularly Yuri because she always knew how to read me.

If she looked deep into my eyes, she'd be able to tell I was hiding something. I couldn't even believe what had just happened. I certainly wasn't ready to talk about it.

"Hey, Dad!" Shelby said into her phone. "Naw, we're about to blow this joint. Probably come home. You on your way there? ... Huh, you're in the parking lot? ... Yeah, we can come out ... Dad, I'm sure whatever you picked is fine ... Okay, we're coming."

Soon as my sister got off of the phone, all of us wanted to know why dad was in the parking lot. We gave Shelby an inquisitive look. She looked back at us like, "Don't ask. Just come on."

Since I always asked questions, I said, "What's going on?"

"Dad's doing something for Mom, so he's got these two pieces of jewelry that the jewelry store loaned him. We can help decide which one she'd like."

Fifteen minutes later, we easily spotted the Town Car that my dad was in. He stepped out of the car, but I could see female legs sitting inside. So I opened the car door, but my dad shut it quickly.

"I'm working on something," he said.

But I'd seen those legs, those perfectly toned and shaped legs. And I remembered the shoes. Miss X was in his limousine. My father showed us two suede jewelry boxes, and when he opened them, my sisters were all goo-goo eyed, and they were arguing over which necklace to pick. I didn't even bother looking.

When they decided on one, he hugged them

and said, "Your mom is going to love this."

"And who's getting the other one?" I said sarcastically.

Looking at me like I was crazy, my dad hesitantly said, "It's going back to the jewelry store. That's where I'm taking it now, and I'm gonna buy this one."

"Yeah, okay," I said rudely.

"What's that supposed to mean?" Shelby asked.

"Dad knows," I said as I looked at him in a way that said I wanted to punch him.

"Dad, we're going to get some pizza. You want to come out with us?" Yuri asked.

He replied, "No, I've got to go to the jewelry store, and I'm still working with a colleague. I won't be in for a while."

"Aw, Dad . . ." Yuri said.

"I know, Joybell. You girls eat though, and get on home," he said.

"We just wish you could come," Yuri told him.

"Yup, trying to get everything in order for January. After the inauguration, I want to get going full speed, so I'm working overtime. I know it's a lot to ask you girls to give up your dad like this, but I've been around so much when we were campaigning, I'm sure you're tired of me now."

I told my sisters I'd be right there, and my dad said, "What's been going on with you?"

"Why can't I get in the limousine?"

"Why'd you need to get in the limousine?"

"That's not what I was asking, Dad. Seems like there's a problem, and I know what it is."

"What?"

"Who's that in there?"

"I just told you and your sisters. I'm working with a colleague."

"Yeah, right, Dad. I guess I'm just disappointed. I thought our family meant more than that to you."

"What are you talking about?"

"Forget it."

"I know it's a lot. I'm secretive about things going on right now, but a lot of this stuff is . . ."

"What, *classified*?" I cut in and said.

"Not necessarily, but isn't everything you

girls want to know? It will reveal itself in time."

"Yeah, but then it might be too late."

"Trust me, baby, I would never let anything harm you or hurt you or our family." He tried to sound reassuring .

"I hear what you're saying, but I'm not sure I believe it."

"I don't know what you're talking about, but relax. Go have fun with your sisters. I hate that I can't be there. Don't wait up."

He kissed me on the cheek, got in the car, and drove away. Playing the good daughter and not confronting him was becoming harder and harder. I didn't know how much longer I could hold it all in.

***

Monday, walking into Marks High School, I was all smiles. Reese and I had been texting back and forth over the weekend. It was simple stuff, but it was cute stuff. We had a connection that was growing. I couldn't wait to see him. He wasn't in the front like usual, so I went on to PE class.

In class, all the girls were mad because we had to run around the track. No one wanted a zero, so we had to get running. I looked at my phone and debated texting Reese. I decided against it. I just planned on seeing him after class. I locked the phone, locked my locker, and took off to the track.

Reese ran through my mind even when I was running. When I saw him, I was going to give him a kiss no matter who was around.

Finally, class was over, and we all needed a shower. I was the first one in. I had a really bad habit of taking long showers. My sisters always got on me at home for doing that. I really couldn't afford to do it at school. For one, other people were waiting to get in the shower, and two, I had to hurry up to get ready to go on to class before I was late. However, for some reason just thinking about Reese made me take a long shower anyway. When I turned on the water, I leaned back. I put my hand on my head and just stood there. I heard a click, and when I opened my eyes I realized time was passing and I was hallucinating.

My sister yelled for me. "Girl, you better come on!"

"Alright, Yuri. I can't believe you let me stay in there that long."

"I didn't know if your cycle started or something, girl, and you needed to wash up."

"Hahaha . . ."

"Hurry up!"

When I dashed out of the shower and went over to the lockers, Trevy was standing there. I had my towel on all tight. I needed her to give me some privacy, but she would not move.

"Trevy, I got to hurry up and get dressed."

"This won't take nothing but a second."

"You heard my sister. She needs to hurry up. We're going to be late," Yuri told her.

Trevy held up her finger. "Real quick."

"Okay, okay. Yes?" I said.

"I just wanted to apologize to you. I feel bad that I was so rude Friday. I really wanted Reese back, but over the weekend I had a chance to think about it, and I'm the one who messed up our relationship. He deserves to try something new, and you seem to like him. So can we be friends?" Trevy stretched out her hand.

"Friends is a stretch," Yuri said to her, sounding like me.

"Yeah, I don't know about all that," I said, holding tight to my towel.

"I just don't think it would be wise for us to be enemies," Trevy said coldly, like there was a double meaning with what she was saying.

"Can we just take it one day at a time?" I asked her.

She went from a frown to a smile. I didn't know how to take that. Was she faking or what?

Trevy said, "Okay, sounds good. You better hurry and get dressed. The bell is going to ring any minute, and nobody wants to miss what's next."

"What's next?" Yuri asked her.

"I think we're having a fire drill."

"How would you know that?" Yuri asked.

"Mr. Hobby just keeps talking to me now. Wonder why, Sloan, huh?"

I knew why. Because she sucked up to him and told him that Reese and I were hot on his tail. My sister walked Trevy out. I didn't have a lot of time to get dressed. Since I had to share a bathroom with my two sisters, I was accustomed to moving quickly. I opened up my locker, and within minutes I was dressed.

Before the bell rung, the fire alarm went off just like Trevy had predicted. We were all outside in a minute, and we were out there for a long time too. With as long as it was taking, we didn't know if this was an actual fire or a drill.

Then people starting looking at me. First, I thought I was being paranoid. But when I looked to the left, I got stares, and when I looked to the right, I got smiles. Once we were told we could go back in, Shelby, Ansli, and Slade came running up to me.

"Oh my gosh, Sloan! Why would you take that?" Shelby yelled as she shook me hard.

I stared at her, confused. Shelby didn't let up.

Shelby said, "Don't play. I know you just thought you sent it to that guy, but guys are trifling."

"What are you talking about?" Yuri asked her.

"Yeah, what are you talking about?" I repeated.

"Just show her!" Ansli said, shaking her head in disgust.

"I don't even know how to," Shelby said.

"You better show her. It's going around," Slade uttered.

Shelby started twiddling with her phone. I grabbed it, and I was appalled to see myself leaning up against the bathroom shower with my head back, a smile on my face, and nothing on my body.

"What, who, huh? How did you get this? Who else has this?" I stuttered.

Yuri leaned in, and as soon as she saw it, I closed the thing, automatically embarrassed. Even though my sisters had seen me bare before, never had it been on a phone and never had it looked like I was posing for *Playboy* or something. What in the world was going on? How did Shelby have this on her phone? Is that why people were looking at me all crazy? Oh my gosh! My eyes started watering up. People were laughing and pointing. Mercifully, the all-clear bell rang. Ansli and Shelby put their arms around me, and we went into the girls' bathroom.

"What happened? Why would you take a selfie like this? And why'd you send it to that boy?" Shelby asked me.

"I didn't take this! How could I? And I didn't send it to anybody! What is going on?" I cried out.

"Well it's been forwarded from Reese's phone to a whole bunch of people."

When she told me that, I just broke down crying. I didn't take a picture of myself nude, and I didn't send it to him. Even if I did, I could not believe he had the gall to send it out to other people. Just when I let my guard down a little bit and trusted him with my heart, he stomped on my sacrifice.

CHAPTER FIVE
SPEECHLESS

My mouth hung open. I couldn't take my eyes off of my own body plastered on the cell phone for the world to see. It was like I was in a trance. I wanted to cry. I wanted to scream, but I was frozen. How did this happen? Clearly, I could see myself in the shower, leaning back and smiling like I was posing. But I did not take a selfie. Though I remember dozing off, dreaming about Reese and imagining us together, I didn't have my phone in the shower, so I could not have done this.

"We're talking to you, Sloan!" Shelby said

after shaking me a bit.

Ansli grabbed my hand to wake me out of my haze and tried to get me to focus. "How did this happen, Sloan?"

"I don't know? Yuri and I just left gym," I said, trying to get my thoughts together. I was starting to choke up.

"Yeah, I don't know either," Yuri said, completely dumbfounded as well.

"Well, I got two problems," Slade said. "One, I can't believe you would take this, but guys can make us do dumb junk. I'm sure you meant it for his eyes only. My second problem is why would he send it out to other people?"

My sister had a great point about Reese selling me out. However, it was hard to focus on that when I was still stuck on how the gross picture got taken and sent to him from my phone. Why was this happening?

"Guys, I didn't take this picture," I tried explaining to my sisters with the utmost sincerity in my eyes.

They couldn't even look at me. I could see the doubt on their faces. Realizing they didn't believe me, I knew I had a big problem. I stared at Yuri. Surely she still had my back.

"If she said she didn't do it, she didn't do it," Yuri explained very unconvincingly to the other three.

"That's all well and good, Yuri, but where was your phone, Sloan?" Shelby asked.

Slade piped in, "Yeah, if you didn't take it in the shower with you, where would it have been, Sis?"

Tired of the interrogation, I yelled, "Locked in the locker!"

Shelby shrugged her shoulders. "Doesn't add up. Are you sure you locked it up?"

"Yes, I am," I uttered, insulted.

"And you have a lock on your phone too, right?" Yuri asked, trying to help me out.

Throwing my hands in the air, I said, "Exactly."

"So if someone would have gotten into the locker, they couldn't have taken a picture on your phone because they don't have a code, right?" Shelby questioned.

Reluctantly, I uttered, "Yeah, right."

Shelby continued, "So then that's why it seems you took the picture, Sloan."

I screamed, "I didn't!"

"Shoot, forget who took the dang photo. We know who sent it to the world. So let's go find him and get some answers . . . I can't believe he sent my sister's picture to all his horny buddies," Slade said.

Ansli added, "That was so unfortunate. Now everyone around here is all excited, forwarding it from here to there to the next person. I thought this guy liked you. How could he do this?"

Slade huffed as we started walking to our next period, "Where is he? Do you know his schedule, Sloan? Talk to us."

I couldn't recall my whole name much less what class Reese was in at that very moment. Plus, the next class hadn't started because the fire drill had thrown the day's schedule off. As fate would have it, Reese was walking toward me all fast and in a hurry like he needed to explain something.

Yuri spotted him too and said, "That's him right there!"

I looked at her and leaned in, "You could have just told me that? Did you have to get our sisters involved?"

"We're involved!" Slade said in a brash tone, overhearing us. "Yeah, we do need to talk to him, Sis, because whatever part of this little prank he thinks is cute, is not."

"Sloan, Sloan, can I talk to you for a second?" Reese said with urgency.

"Urgh no! You're going to talk to all of us!" Slade insisted.

"Yeah!" Shelby cut in. "How could you do that to my sister?"

"People are coming up to me, asking the exact same thing!" he said to them. "But can I talk to Sloan?"

"I don't have anything to say to you," I cut in and said. "How could you do this to me?"

"I can't even believe you sent me the picture!" Reese declared in an appalled voice.

"So because she sent you the picture, that gave you the okay to send it out to everybody in America?" Slade asked him.

"Oh my gosh, this is going to ruin daddy's

reputation, and he's not even mayor yet," I said, turning away and wishing I could hide under the school building.

Slade popped me in the head, "It's messing up your reputation. Focus on that right now, girl."

Looking at Slade like she was crazy, I gasped, "I get that; that's not what I'm saying at all."

"Hey, y'all listen, I didn't even do this," Reese said.

"You didn't do what? Cause my sister embarrassment like you have?" Shelby asked.

"Yes, darn right. I'm saying I didn't forward this." He stepped to me and said, "I can't explain how this got out. Think about it though. I wouldn't want any of these guys around here looking at you like that. I'm surprised that you would send it to me even."

"I didn't send it to you," I quickly let him know.

"Yeah, you did. It came to my phone from your number," he said.

I shouted back, "No, I didn't!"

"I don't know what world the two of you

guys are living in," Shelby said. "Or you might just think I'm stupid."

Slade snatched the phone from my hand and said, "We aren't stupid. The evidence is here. Y'all might want to play all innocent and act like you don't know how this happened, but the proof says how it happened. Sloan, you clearly wanted to entice this guy, and Ryan, Roger, Reese, or whatever your name is . . . you thought you were all that for a girl to send you such a picture, so you showed the world. Quit insulting our intelligence, and own up to this debacle."

I couldn't speak for Reese, but I was telling the truth about me. It did seem awfully suspicious that he was saying the same exact thing that I was. I got that my sisters thought we were guilty. What other explanation was there for how all this happened. Reese had to have sent it out to his boys who forwarded it out to others. The look on his face showed me he felt bad, and if he felt bad, was that an admission to guilt?

"Talk to me, please," he pleaded.

I was so frustrated. I just threw up my hands and said, "I ain't got nothing to say."

I walked away, feeling worse than I ever had. I was a disgrace to my family. Shoot, I was a disgrace to myself.

***

Not even fifteen minutes later, I was sitting in the office. I had gone to my class, and my teacher wouldn't even let me in. She told me I was being summoned to the office. It didn't take a rocket scientist to figure out I was in trouble for sexting. At some point you get tired of trying to explain your way through the madness, and you just accept whatever fate was coming your way.

The door to the office opened, and Reese walked in. He was told to have a seat as well. He sat down at the empty seat next to me.

I turned away and said, "Please sit over there."

He complied. I didn't want to talk to him. I didn't want to hear his lies because the more I thought about it, what guy wouldn't want to brag that a girl thought so much of him that she'd be willing to send him her assets? If that guy had any sense, he'd share the photo so his stock would go up.

I guess that's just what got me about Reese. I didn't think he cared about trying to please guys and be popular. I thought he was his own man, not caring what peers he impressed. I guess I was wrong.

Dr. Garner came out of his office and called for me to follow him. He said hello, but he wasn't even looking at me. When we got to the office, he couldn't even look my way. Clearly, he was embarrassed about what he'd just seen. The picture had gotten all the way to the principal in less than an hour. I was so in trouble. There was no way I was going to be able to explain this to my dad. Ironically, out of all of my sisters, I knew my father would think I would be the least likely to mess up in this way.

"Sloan, I, I, I, I just can't believe what I'm seeing here," Dr. Garner said, stuttering "But you know we can't have this, and as much as it pains me, I called your parents. You're going to be suspended."

"You haven't even asked my side of the story,

sir," I uttered, needing to speak out now.

"When I have evidence like this, young lady, that's sent from your phone, unfortunately this unflattering selfie, as you young people call it, is all the proof I need. This has got to die down around here. I've got to set some ground rules so that everyone understands forwarding this type of material is criminal. I'm sure you saw Reese out front. As a young man who's a leader in this school, working with my parent group and my teachers to make sure that this school has everything it needs, I'm disappointed in him too. You wait here for your mom. I'm going to talk to him separately. While I don't condone you taking this kind of picture and sending it to him, I certainly have an issue with him sending it to others as well. I'll be back in just a second."

Dr. Garner got up and went out the door. I started hitting my head. This was a nightmare, and I wanted to wake up.

When the door opened, I just knew it was my folks. I turned and got a knot in my stomach, seeing the assistant principal, Mr. Hobby. The smirk plastered on his face creeped me out.

Mr. Hobby said, "Well, well, well, what do we have here? Somebody trying to accuse me of doing wrong and the very next week, you're the laughingstock of the school."

"Sir, are you supposed to be saying all this to me right now?" I said.

"Seeing the picture I saw, saying something to you isn't what I'm thinking about. I just got to be honest." He licked his crusty lips.

"Sir!" I yelled. I never imagined wanting to pose for *Playboy*. I didn't have any desire to. I thought it was absolutely disgusting, but sometimes you find yourself in places you never thought you'd end up. I could see what it felt like being someone who had a great job, lost it, and the next thing he knows . . . he's homeless. Or a teenager falling in love, getting too close to a guy, and the next thing you know . . . she's pregnant. Or one of the brightest girls at school minding her own business, and the next thing you know . . . she's the laughingstock of the school because everybody's seen places she hasn't even examined on her own body.

Mr. Hobby left me to wallow in my pity.

The next voices I heard were that of my mom and Dr. Garner coming into the office. She didn't give me a chance to explain. She didn't look at me either. They were talking all around me.

Dr. Garner told her, "Yes, kids make mistakes. Yes, even the brightest children do things that their parents aren't expecting sometimes. I hate to give her these three days."

"Well, with everything she just did, trust me, she can use three days," my mother told him.

I could tell steam was piping out of my mom's ears, but she was playing her role with Dr. Garner. She was being all nice and chummy, talking about how excited she was for my father and all his great plans for the city. Yet there her daughter sat embarrassing the heck out of the family. She wasn't cool with that. I knew it. Finally, when we were in the car, I was ready for her to let me have it, but she drove in silence with an angry look on her face.

"Say something, Mom. Tell me. What is it that you want to say? Or you want to let me have it even though you haven't even heard me out," I demanded.

Finally, she broke. "Hear you out? Sloan, are you serious? I have to look at my daughter's bare body on a phone! First of all, why you would even think this is okay? To take a picture of yourself and send it to some boy is just crazy. I knew your sisters were talking about guys, but you assured us, 'My head is focused. I'm not even thinking about guys. All I want to do is graduate top of my class.' Yet here you are doing something way worse than anybody in this family ever has!"

"So you're perfect?" I said in an angry tone.

"I didn't say I was perfect, but I'm your mother, and I never took naked pictures of myself and thought it was okay."

"Well, I didn't either, Mom!"

"So now you're in denial? That's just great, Sloan. That's just great! You had a dream of Harvard. You had a vision to be top of your class. Why couldn't you just stay focused?" When we got to the red light, she looked over at me and said, "I know I've been working hard at the firm on this food poisoning case. Obviously, I need to pay more attention to my child. So if you want me to apologize, then I'll do that."

Really pissed at this point, I said, "No, Mom. You need to pay more attention to your marriage."

Squinting her eyes she said, "What are you talking about, Sloan?"

"I'm talking about you all mad at me about little pictures that you saying that I sent . . ."

"You sent? I'm not talking hearsay that you sent it. Dear, I've got the proof! You sent it, okay! What are you talking about, about my marriage?"

The last thing I wanted to do was hurt my mom, but she was hurting me by not even giving me a chance to explain, by not even asking me what was really up, by not trusting me. I wasn't lying. She knew that I wasn't a liar, so I reached inside my purse and pulled out the picture that Mr. Brown had given me and showed it to my mom. She snatched it out of my hand, and as tears welded up in her eyes, she had nothing else to say from that point on. As bad as I felt about my own situation, I now felt way worse for breaking her heart. She being way too hard on me though. What else was a girl to do?

***

I wanted to snatch the picture out of my mom's hands and pretend I'd never shown it to her, but what was done was done. I could see she was not only confused but hurt as well. She didn't grill me more about how I got it. She didn't want to discuss it either. We simply rode the rest of the way home without a word spoken.

She didn't have to tell me I was grounded. She didn't have to tell me to go to my room. She didn't have to tell me I was on punishment. I knew my fate. Even though I wanted some alone time, a part of me wanted to hug her and reassure that it had to be more to the story than what we saw in the photo. However, even if she gave me the time of day, I couldn't give her the answers that would give her comfort because I really believed, deep down, that my dad was engaging in some type of uncouth relationship with the mystery chick.

Later that evening, I heard a whole bunch of arguing. The walls were trembling because of the yelling going on. I peeked my head out into the hallway and looked over the steel railing.

"So you mean to tell me you don't know where she got this from?" my mother questioned my dad.

"No, I don't know where she got it from, but I'm telling you it doesn't mean anything," my father replied.

My mom retorted with attitude, "Funny, seeing you all locked up in somebody's arms like you're whispering sweet nothings in her ear doesn't look like nothing to me."

"Shh, hon, keep your voice down. The girls are upstairs."

"And with my daughters talking to boys, they need to know there are trifling men in the world. Sometimes you can't trust none of them," my mom said as she rolled her eyes at my dad.

"Aw, baby, don't be like that," he said as he tried to wrap his arms around her.

Pulling away, she said, "Well, you're not telling me any details. I'm supposed to trust that it's nothing? That it's not what I see?"

"It's nothing. It's not what it looks like," he said as he followed my mom around to the foyer of the house.

I went around the corner and saw all four of my sisters perched on the stairs, looking over. My parents must have known we were there. They stepped into my dad's office.

"Where did Mom get a picture from?" Slade asked.

"Need to ask Sloan," Shelby said with a bit of anger in her voice.

"I can't do this right now. I just can't take this." We heard my mom scream out. "Please, don't touch me. Sleep in the guest room."

My mom fled out of the office. She looked up at us, and we saw watery eyes. She went into her bedroom and slammed the door.

My dad came out of his office. He picked up his keys and went out the garage door, slamming it behind him. My sisters turned to me, looking at me like I was evil.

"What did you do?" Shelby said in an accusatory voice.

Not afraid of any of them, I responded, "I was with Momma, and she was talking about me and that I needed to get myself together. I didn't want her thinking that I was the only one who had issues. She had issues too."

"So you just gon' give her a picture? I mean what was all on it?" Ansli asked.

"I tried to tell you guys. Y'all don't want to listen to me. She needs to know. Dad is cheating. He can stand here and act like everything is okay when it's not okay."

"How do you know that for sure?" Yuri asked me. "You want us to believe you didn't take that selfie of yourself, so if Dad has some picture where it looks like he's in some relationship with another lady, maybe there is another explanation."

Slade jumped in and said, "Yeah, you should have found that out before you just assumed and gave it to Mom."

"You could be messing up our whole family over nothing," Ansli said.

"I didn't think it was nothing. If there was no explanation to it, then why doesn't Mom believe him? She's an attorney, for goodness sake. She investigates with the best of them. If she's not believing what he's saying, it's probably because she knows her husband. Maybe he's been smelling like unknown perfume. Maybe some of the late nights really can't be explained. I don't know, but she needed to know what I know. I don't apologize for that."

"Well, you need to," Shelby said, giving me a look that cut like a knife.

"Until you have all the facts yourself, you should have kept your mouth shut. This isn't just about you. This is our family too. And it might be okay for you to go around half-cocked, but the gun has gone off, and it looks like you've blown a hole through our family. That's not okay with me, Sis. I love you to pieces, but you always think you know everything. You don't. You're the one who's the joke. You're the one who's suspended, and you're the one who messed up our parents' relationship, probably over nothing. I mean, don't get it twisted. Dad is a fine-looking brother with a bunch of power. There's going to be a whole bunch of women coming at him, but

Dad's got way too much to lose for him to get with some trick," Slade added.

"But you're so naive, and you think you're so smart," Shelby said as she came close to my face. "The only thing you've done is ruin everything. Mom didn't need you to fix her problems. You can't even fix your own. Gosh, sometimes I hate you!"

My sister had said she loved me in the past, but the way she said she hated me seemed more real. She turned around and left, and so did her three other goons. Even Yuri left my side. I was left standing there to contemplate. Yes, I still believed my dad had done something wrong, but they made a good point. The world thought I had done something wrong too, and I hadn't. So had I gotten this all twisted for nothing? Just thinking that I could be wrong left me speechless.

CHAPTER SIX
SEEK

My three days at home suspended from school seemed like the longest three days of my life. While my parents had seemed to work out whatever it was going on between them, my sisters hadn't forgiven me, and I don't know if my dad was so upset with me that I was crossed off his list or if he was just so busy that he hadn't had a chance to come and deal directly with me himself.

But the morning I was to go back to school, my dad said, "Hey, I'm taking you." It actually was fine with me because I didn't want to ride with my sisters. I could always depend on Yuri to side with me, but now she was hanging out with Slade more than me. Certainly my mom knew my dad better than I did, and if she was okay with him now, maybe I did need to cut him some slack.

"Listen, Sloan. I know I've been going in so many diffcrent directions, but I am not at all pleased with these stunts you're pulling to get attention."

All I could do was cross my arms and huff. I wasn't trying to get attention.

My dad continued, "You don't have to harm your reputation to try to get people to notice you. You're a beautiful girl. I know it's hard because your sisters are too. A lot of people are looking at our family, but you've got so much going on for yourself. I don't need you to make up lies or—"

"Okay, okay, Dad. Enough." I said "Mr. Brown gave me the picture," I said.

"Brown?"

"Yes, the day of the election. I didn't know everything going on with you and that lady.

Then I saw her in the limousine at the football game last week, and a couple of other times I've seen her whispering in your ear. I even saw her calling your phone one time. It seems really suspect to me, that's all."

"I can't explain all that to you."

"Why, Dad? If it's nothing to tell, why can't you talk to me?"

"Because it's not your place, Sloan. I know you're growing up, but baby you ain't grown. I'm just real sad and disappointed that I've got to see my daughter showing her body for all the world to see. I mean who is this guy you sent this thing to? You like him that much? You ready to have sex? You know the ramifications of putting yourself out there like that? Some guy might see this and want you—rape you or something. I mean it's just senseless, Sloan."

"Dad, I didn't do this."

"I know you didn't make the guy send it out to other people."

"No, I didn't even take it of myself and send it to him. Like you said, I have too much self-worth to do anything that stupid."

"Then how did he get it?"

I just looked out the window. I didn't have an answer. I had been pondering over that question for over the last three days, playing all of the events over and over in my head, and still I came up with no explanation. My phone had a lock on it; plus, it was locked in my locker. When I got back from the shower, it was protected where I put it, though I didn't look at it to see my recent pictures.

"If you said you didn't do it, Sloan, then we need to figure out what happened."

"Just forget it, Dad. I've already done my time."

"I've got to go in and talk to the principal, anyway. Was it other stuff going on at the school that I need to address? Anybody bullying you? Pressuring you? Anything?"

"It's lots of stuff going on at the school, but don't worry about it."

"If I wasn't worried about it, Sloan, I wouldn't ask. Obviously, I care." My dad was trying to get information, but I was so past it all at that point.

When we got to school, we had to go straight

to the principal's office. My time was up. I didn't understand why I had to be summoned again, but the counselor was there. Everybody wanted to make sure I was okay and that I understood how I was hurting myself by sexting.

***

It was like I was transparent. Everybody was looking at me like they could see through my clothes—I guess because of the images that were floating around out there. I guess they could. I was trying to find enough strength to keep my head up high. I was thankful I had four escorts.

"We're not going to let you walk through all these stares and sneers without backup." Slade looked over at me and said.

"Yeah, if they got something to say about my sister, they're gonna have to deal with me." Shelby added.

Ansli and Yuri put both of their arms in mine. I didn't want to smile, but I couldn't help it when I saw Yuri making goofy faces. She always cracked me up. She leaned in and said, "I need you to forgive me."

"What, you believe me now?"

"No, but it shouldn't matter. We're young. I shouldn't be mad at you because of your choices. Okay—well, maybe I should be mad at you, but I shouldn't stay mad at you."

"Yeah, keep y'all's sister covered up! Because she certainly won't do it herself!" one guy yelled.

"All y'all gon' strip down? I can take the picture!" somebody else yelled. I wanted to scream. I guess I was getting antsy, but my sisters kept me composed. I didn't think I needed them. I thought I was fine with them hating me, but they got me through those moments. When I got to my class, I had to come face-to-face with Reese, the culprit who had turned my dream into a nightmare, and he had the nerve to ask if he could talk to me.

"That would be a no!" Slade said to him. "Sis, go sit down. Don't say nothing to this jerk."

"You all need to get on to class," my AP World History teacher said to my sisters. Mr. Bonner leaned in and said, "I don't know what you and Reese are into, but I'm not tolerating any foolishness in my class."

"I'm not even speaking to him, sir," I said.

"Oh, so it's like that? I text you, and you don't text me back—" Reese said as he came up behind me.

"I don't have my phone! I wonder why?" I said to him. "I don't wanna hear anything you have to say." If I was only annoyed with Reese trying to chum up to me, I was furious with Mr. Bonner because he was still giving the students answers. It was something to coach your students, but it was another thing to not make your students earn their grades. I had started out the month of November thankful for so much, but now half of it was gone, and it was hard to find one thing I was happy about. But then I leaned back in my chair and thought about my sisters. When I needed them most, they were there. That counted for something.

***

The next day I had to go to journalism class. I walked straight to Ms. Spears and said, "Can I please talk to you for a second?"

"Sure." She got up from her desk, and we

stepped into her office.

"I know you know what's happened to me. It's breaking news, after all."

"I'd love to hear your story. I don't believe everything I hear," she said, which was actually pretty comforting. I think she was the first person who had said that to me throughout this whole ordeal.

"It doesn't matter. I just came to tell you that I wanted to turn in my resignation. I don't deserve to be on your paper. I can turn in my notes for the article that I was working on. You can tell it's a clear conflict of interest now to finish it with the scandal between me and the guy that I was researching."

Ms. Spears shook her head. "Well, I don't know you, Sloan, but I think I know you well enough to know when something that drastic happens, there's more to the story."

"I don't want to do anything to damage the reputation of the paper. And with me being attached, you'll be taking a lot of heat."

"Okay, so why aren't you telling me your version of the story?"

"Because I've been trying for so long to tell people that what they see isn't real. I mean, yes, it's my body, sent from my phone to this guy, but I didn't send it to him. It's frustrating."

"To me it doesn't look like you took a selfie."

"Huh? Excuse me?" I said really confused.

"Now, we were all told to delete the picture, but because I wanted to talk to you about this, I have it. I'm not going to look at it with you, but notice how your arm that is not on your head is down. You don't see your hand, so it could be a selfie, but the position wouldn't give the same angle on the camera. I have a strong gut feeling someone else took this."

Quickly, I looked at the picture, and she was right. How had I not seen that before? I always thought that it was weird that in the picture my eyes were closed, and I looked like I was dreaming. I remember doing that, but I hadn't taken this picture, and that was the first bit of proof. "But how could they have taken it with my camera?"

"I was hoping you would be able to fill in that part."

"No, because one, I have a lock on it, and two, it was locked in my locker." Only my sisters know the combination to my phone. Yuri has gym with me, but she would never do this."

"Are you sure?" my teacher asked me.

"I'm 105 percent sure."

"I don't think you can ever rule out anybody, but I certainly wouldn't want to think that your sister did this either. But it does look like there's more to the story here, and a good journalist would find out what it is. I'm not happy this happened to you, but I think some good can come of it."

"What are you talking about? I'm absolutely humiliated!"

"Right, but you'll have a different empathy than you didn't have before when you're researching cases. Now you're on the other end of the scandal. That's something no one can teach you."

"Empathy?"

"Yes, it's like you have on glasses now. Glasses of journalist humanity. This is going to make you so much better. You've always been a smart, savvy writer, but when you throw heart into the mix and dig to get the truth out of every story, shedding new light on what you're reporting and making the reader feel what you feel, you're doing great reporting. That's where you're headed—that's where you can go. I believe in you, Sloan. I always have, but there's been something missing. And it was that tough exterior that nobody could tell you anything. Now you've been beat up a little bit, so much so that you were willing to quit something you're good at. But now you'll be excellent because this happened, and when you find out the truth, you'll get your reputation back."

"You seem confident. I didn't know you cared like that."

"Oh yeah. I'm hard on you because you could be great. I'm not supposed to sit here and let my best student give me poor efforts. No."

"Where do I start? It's not like I have any friends who have evidence that can show me who put their hands on my stuff. I don't even have my phone."

"When you concentrate on the fact that you know you didn't take this picture, you'll find your way to the truth."

I gave her the biggest hug. For the first time in a long time, I had something I'd been missing, and that was hope. She'd given me back my life. All I had to do was dig. So what I was in a hole? Now was time to crawl out of it. I was a victim, but now it was time for me to be my own hero.

***

It was Thanksgiving time, and the Sharp family had lots to celebrate. My dad was mayor-elect. Shelby's fashions were getting great reviews. Ansli's photography business was extremely profitable. Slade had a hit song, and my mom was working hard on her food poisoning case. Nobody really expected Yuri and me to do too much yet because we were the babies of the family, but my sweet sixteen was coming up at the end of December. I couldn't be too happy when I still hadn't found out any information about who took the picture. I was happy, however, to see my maternal grandparents and my mother's younger sister, Sadie.

While we were sitting down for dinner, I saw Dad check his cell phone, and then he got up and was gone for five minutes. I wondered if he was talking to Miss X, who was supposed to be nothing. But when he got up for a second time later on when we were about to start eating dessert, I got up, followed him, and stood on the outside of his door. I heard him say, "You know I can't talk to you about this right now." Why was he getting so hostile? Why couldn't the person respect that he was with his family? Probably because it was someone with whom he had an unhealthy relationship. The person didn't understand boundaries and didn't know where his or her place was. As much as I wanted my family to be whole, I knew it was still really broken.

"What you doin' eavesdropping?" Aunt Sadie said to me.

I was so startled. "I'm not. I was getting something."

"You better get away from that door. Come

on up here. Let's talk. Your sisters will be up in just a second."

After our big dinner, I was thankful that my parents had enough means to hire a catering company because they were the ones who cleaned up. All my sisters came upstairs to talk to Aunt Sadie. She was working on her doctorate at Duke, but she also danced as a Carolina Panthers cheerleader. She was smart and sassy. Anytime we told her our problems, before she was gone, she'd solve them.

"So you know I know what's going on with you, right?"

"The world knows what's going on with me. Please tell me no one sent you the picture."

"Yeah, I got it. I thought your head had been photoshopped on it at first. No way would my niece do something like that. So what's the story behind all this?"

"That's what I'm trying to figure out."

"If you didn't take the picture and send it to the guy and the guy's been trying to tell you he didn't send it to other people, then you gotta think about who had the most to gain out of y'all's demise."

"I don't understand what you mean," I said to her.

"If some other guy liked you, it seems odd that he would make you look that bad. So it's gotta be some girl who liked him." When she said that, the name Trevy just kept ringing loud in my ear.

"But I don't even know how she could pull off something like this."

"So there is a girl who liked him?"

"Yeah, real strong, real tough, real hard. All of that."

"Then it's her. Someway, somehow she did it or had somebody else do it. She wanted to bring you and this guy down. You should talk to him."

"He probably knows the whole story. He was trying to tell me something."

"And what did he say?"

"I didn't want to hear it."

"Uh! Girl!"

"I thought he sent my picture out to the world!"

"Yeah, but anyway that was definitely what

she wanted; for y'all to be as far apart from each other. I'm telling you it's her. I might not be able to tell you how. You want to be a news reporter. Figure out the details."

"You know my teacher just told me the same thing the other day."

"And what have you done about it?"

"I've been trying to think through it. I have a pass code on my phone and my phone was locked up and I knew Yuri didn't do it. So, I just can't figure it out."

"Well, talk to the guy. This isn't the end of life. I know you're not going to be able to erase this picture, and it can pop up anywhere. But as cute as you are, girl, being known as a sex symbol—let's just say that there could be worse things."

"Ooh, Aunt Sadie!"

"I'm just keeping it real!"

I went to Yuri's room and asked her if I could use her iPad. When she said yes, I went back to my room, shut the door, and tried to FaceTime Reese. He didn't answer, so I went downstairs and had dessert. My mom pulled me into an embrace and said, "Whatever crazy thing your aunt said to you, forget it." We both smiled. We'd come a long way, and the last thing I wanted was for my father to hurt her. I had to find out what was going on between him and Miss X, but I did have my own business to tend to, so I quickly ate a slice of sweet potato pie, washed some dishes, and went upstairs to call Reese again.

He picked up and said, "Yeah?"

"Hey."

"What do you want? I just picked up to tell you to quit calling me."

"I know I'm probably the last person you want to talk to."

"Yeah, you for sure are. Honestly, as if I didn't feel bad enough about everything that happened, the fact that you didn't even believe me or give me a chance to explain sucks. So you know, I'm over it now. Nothing else to say."

"Well, wait. I wanna ask questions. I wanna know what happened. You've been wanting to talk to me, so certainly you know more than I do."

"Because you wouldn't give me the time of day and formed your own conclusions, condemning me with the rest of the world, don't even come to me. I don't have the answers you seek."

CHAPTER SEVEN
SWEETHEART

"Please talk to me," I said to Reese when I called him back.

"It's Thanksgiving and all, Sloan. I'm with my family today. I don't have nothing else to say."

"If you cared for me at all, you would—" I said before Reese cut me off.

"Wait, let me just stop you right there," he said. "I cared for you a lot. But I mean, there's only so much a guy can take."

"How do you think I felt these last days? My picture was sent everywhere from your phone. I thought you were the one who did it."

"I get that the evidence pointed to me, but when you said you didn't send the shot to me, I believed you. Why was it so hard for you to do the same for me?" Reese asked as he looked down and paused for a second. "Don't get me wrong, if I would have seen it, I would've been flattered. I would have known it was for my eyes only. I ain't sayin' I would have erased it, but I wouldn't have wanted anyone else to see the goods. I actually deleted it from several phones. I was so angry."

I could imagine Reese snatching people's phones and deleting it. He was the protective type. How could I have been so judgmental?

Peering directly into the camera, he said, "I thought I was clear. I've liked you all year. I act tough, but I had to get up the nerve to talk to you. I wouldn't do anything to hurt you."

"So can you help me get to the bottom of all this, then? I'm the laughingstock, Reese."

"My reputation is trashed too. They're thinking about pressing criminal charges, and it hurt me bad that you thought I hurt you."

"I was wrong, and I'm trying to prove it. I've been doing a little digging on my own, and I've got some theories. Nothing I can prove just yet, but I can't get your old girl to crack."

"You think it's Trevy, don't you?"

"You do too?"

"She would've had the most to gain. Also, I know she wasn't real happy when she found out I liked you. Everybody thought I sent those pictures to everybody else, but she was awfully sympathetic, like she knew for sure I didn't do it."

"It wasn't fair that I had doubts," I told him.

"That's just the thing. I wanted you to hear me out. But let's figure this out. I've been trying to get Trevy to crack, and she's smart. She's not telling me nothing."

"Well, thanks for telling me. And I'm sorry I didn't hear you out."

"That's all I wanted you to say," he said, showing me his perfect smile before we said good night.

Yuri came into my room. I handed her the iPad. Before she left, she stared at me.

"Who were you talking to?" she asked.

"Reese," I uttered, unable to lie to her.

"No, Sloan! Not that guy!"

"He didn't do it."

"What are you talking about?"

I grabbed her empty hand and squeezed it. "Listen, I didn't take the picture of myself and send it to him, and he didn't receive it and send it out to a whole bunch of guys. It just didn't happen that way. Somehow Trevy had something to do with it."

"Now, that's a story I believe," Yuri said, surprising me with her support.

"Why?" I asked, happy that she believed the theory. I needed to figure this out.

"Because she's always looking at you crazy, like she wanted to scratch your eyes out or something. And she looks at him like she wants to have sex with him in front of the world or something. I don't know. She was just eerie. She tried to act like she was your friend, but I could see through it all. You didn't want to hear me. Did you ever let her use your phone?"

"She asked to see it one day at the football game."

"And did you let her?"

"I can't remember," I said as I thought back. "No, I didn't. She had hers on her all the time."

"She didn't know she had her phone on her? See, that's just weird."

"But she did ask me to unlock mine before she found hers."

"So she could've gotten your code then."

"Yeah, but I never thought she knew my code because she didn't use the phone. So I can't really verify if she saw it or not."

Pacing back and forth, Yuri said, "Oh, you can verify."

Frustrated, I sighed, fell onto my bed, and said, "Maybe I just want to pin this on somebody else so badly . . ."

"You want the truth, and if she did this, it changes everything."

"But how are we gonna prove it?"

Yuri shrugged her shoulders. She came over and pulled me up. When she threw her arms around me, I instantly felt better.

"I miss our talks," I said to her. "Let's not stay away from each other again. You didn't believe me."

"Well, you kicked me out every time I wanted to change that. So, next time I know to keep pushing."

"Yeah," I told her. "We need each other."

"We sure do."

***

The next school day, as people were going into the gym, Yuri pulled me to the side and said, "I just got her. Let's go to the office. I taped Trevy spilling the beans on how and why she framed you!"

"What do you mean you have her?" I asked.

Yuri played me a recording of Trevy confessing to everything. She bragged to some girls that she was behind the whole thing because she didn't like them giving me credit for my growing popularity. She said I didn't do anything to deserve all the notoriety. Not only did she know the password to my phone, but she knew the combination to my locker.

I remember us getting dressed in the same places and her watching me. I didn't know she was looking at what number I put into the lock. She also turned off my flash and put my phone on silent. So when she took the picture, I was none the wiser. She already had Reese's phone. She knew he never used his at school, so he didn't even know it was missing. She sent it to him, then sent it out from his phone, put his phone back in his book bag, and when Reese got called out for being the sexting culprit, he didn't even know he possessed the proof.

"Oh my gosh, Yuri, oh my gosh!" I hugged her tight.

The two of us told our gym teachers where we were going and ran to see Dr. Garner. Yuri had also called our parents, and when the recording was played for them, Trevy was escorted off the school property in handcuffs.

"Please can you call Reese, please?" I insisted.

Dr. Garner got Reese out of class. When he came into the office and saw all the people and a police car through the glass in the front of the school, fear set on his face. He thought he was in more trouble. I rushed up to him and hugged him so tight.

"Trevy did do it," I took his hand and turned him toward everyone so they could apologize to us both.

Reese didn't care about any of that. Yeah, it was good to get his name cleared, but more than anything, he was happy I truly knew he didn't set out to hurt me. He cared more about my feelings than his own. Reese was a guy worth keeping.

***

"This Is My Story: A Student's Tale" by Sloan Sharp. I couldn't believe I was reading those words in the *Charlotte Observer*. It was thanks to the reporter I met at the debate who gave me some water. Once the debate was over, she wanted to make sure I was okay. She also gave me her card and told me I could submit anything. I was happy to get this. I just wanted her to look over it and give me her thoughts. I never thought it'd be published.

My words read:

Being the sharpest knife in the drawer comes with great responsibility. Whenever you're pulled out, you're expected to deliver and be on the cutting edge of things. But what happens when someone comes and dulls your world? Well, that's what happened to me. I'm the mayor-elect's daughter, and many would think my world is perfect right about now. In less than two months, my father will be taking the oath of office to run the great city of Charlotte.

Out of my five sisters, I'm known as the brain. I have a 4.0 GPA, and I've never given my parents much worry. However, when someone decided my education wasn't that important to me and that my reputation needed to be tarnished, she took advantage of a girl's innocence. I'm telling my story because I want the city to know all of us young people aren't bad.

We are young. We do get into mischief, but we need adults to help keep us on the right track. We need parents to parent their children so that they understand they don't have to be jealous of what somebody else has. Stay in your lane, run your own race and be your own knife. Don't cut anyone off at the legs. We all have good in us. We just have to decide to be good all the time.

I've always been a private school girl, but I love attending Marks High. There's something about the hodgepodge of people coming together for the collective cause of being educated that makes me tick. But like every great thing, there're still some nooks and crannies that need to be cleaned out.

Teachers, I understand that this profession is a job, but do it well all the time. Grade hard so your kids can do well on tests. Don't give them the answers so they fish for a day. When you truly educate them, they can fish for a lifetime. School board members, what's up with no textbooks?

As I said earlier, I've been fortunate to do pretty well in school. I work at it, but textbooks help me. When I don't have them, I'm handicapped.

Summing up my story, I'm a Sharp girl who is on the ball—most of the time. To all the teens in the city, let's be better. Let's demand more, and let's go get ours. If we don't enjoy our youth, we'll have nobody to blame but ourselves. Life isn't always fair, but everything you go through can make you wiser, stronger, and better.

The phone was ringing off the hook at my house. People loved my article, and actually, my parents were pretty proud. When Ms. Spears told me she was proud of me, I truly felt accomplished. My parents and the principal wanted to know exactly what I was talking about in terms of teachers helping students out on tests. While I only knew of one, it turned out there were a couple of others in the school not doing their job either. They were all dismissed.

The school board put on their agenda to address the textbook issue. Lots of students said they were going to show up for the meeting in December to voice their concerns. Some parents claimed they didn't even know we didn't have books.

When my phone rang and I saw it was Reese, my hands started shaking. "So you got my text message with my new number, huh?" I said.

"I did. I also read your article. It's good. You made a difference."

"About time I did something right," I said, still feeling bad I condemned him like people did me.

"Well, it's time for us to move past that. We've got a playoff game tomorrow. If you're up for it, I'd love for you to help me in the booth again." He must've heard me laughing, cooing, and smiling through the phone because he said, "I guess that's a yes."

It took forever for the game to begin. Reese and I were perched right beside our assistant principal again. I couldn't believe we had to be close to the jerk.

Reese saw him rolling his eyes our way, and Reese leaned in and said, "What I really liked about your article even more than the apology, was the fact that you said some things right. But you and I both know that there's still something wrong at our school. We need to deal with it."

"You think he's still stealing money? He didn't get caught."

"You started cleaning house. We might as well take care of him too," Reese said as I nodded.

My sisters came by and told Reese they were sorry as well. He seemed to really appreciate that. He was being so sweet. He understood how we could have gotten it all mixed up.

When halftime was approaching, we shut down the PTSA booth. We told the assistant principal good-bye, and when he thought we were gone, we went around the back of the concession stand. Just as he thought no one was looking, he started counting the money in the box. That was innocent enough until he took a few twenties and stashed them in his pocket. Reese recorded it all on his cell phone.

We didn't have to go far to look for Dr. Garner. He actually found us. "What are you two doing back here in the dark with a cell phone?"

We said nothing. We just played the recording. The police who were on the premises to watch the game ushered our assistant principal away in handcuffs.

My eyes spotted a Town Car. My face showed I was upset. Was my dad at the school again with Miss X?

Reese touched me and asked, "What's wrong? You can talk to me. You can tell me anything. I want you to be my girl."

I blushed and stroked his cheek letting him know I wanted that too. However, this was my family's personal business. I couldn't let Reese into my thoughts. Saying what I felt comfortable sharing, I said, "What do you do when you feel like your family is falling apart?"

"After what we just went through? Even if it is, you can handle it," Reese said as he moved my hair out of my face from the blowing wind.

I gave him a big hug. Reese was a motivator. He certainly had pumped me up. I had to keep digging. I had to find the truth, and whatever it was, it wasn't going to break me.

Reese and I walked back over to our high

school stadium. The fourth quarter was ending, and we won the game. We were at a new school, but we were fierce competitors. Mavericks to the end. I need to incorporate that mantra in my life.

***

"So everybody thinks this is all okay to get all dressed up to go to some party for Daddy?" I asked Yuri. I was still having my doubts about my dad's fidelity.

"Come on, Sloan," Yuri said as she turned her back so I could zip her up. "Dad's about to be the next mayor. Lots of people want to give him parties now. You gotta be excited for him and help him celebrate as we escort him to the first gala."

"Isn't he throwing this party?" I questioned, getting my sister to see what she was saying held no merit.

"Okay, listen to this song," Slade rushed into the room and said, not caring that we were in the middle of a conversation.

Once she started the music, my head started

bopping. She and her singing partner, Charlotte, had cut their first demo. The sound was off the chain.

Slade bragged, "Dad said we can sing at the party tonight! We're going to perform this, but I wanted you two to tell me what you think. And you've got to see Mom. Shelby designed her the prettiest dress, and the lady Shelby works with actually had it made. Mom looks stunning."

"Oh, and let me guess," I said a little peeved that everybody was so into this whole party. "Ansli is taking pictures tonight!"

"Yeah, maybe you could write about it. Put it in the society column or something," Slade said, not at all sensing I thought this was crazy.

I couldn't tell whether my sister was serious or not about me writing a story on a darn party. I knew she wanted the spotlight, but didn't my sister sense I wasn't feeling it. We were playing family. I didn't want to spend my night smiling when I knew I had reason to frown.

The two of them were super excited. Their giddiness was getting on my nerves. I walked back into my room after getting tired of standing in front of the mirror, primping with my sisters, and I called Reese.

"What's going on?" he asked. "You calling to say you'll be my girl?"

Smiling through the phone, I said, "Thought my body language had already told you, but if you must hear me say it...yes, I'll be your girl."

"That's what's up," he said in a overjoyed tone. "What's going on?"

"I don't wanna go to this party 'cause I don't trust my dad."

"You didn't tell me everything going on, and I'm not gonna guess. I will say that maybe it's different from what you think."

"Maybe I didn't get suspended this year," I sarcastically said. "But I did."

"So what'd you call me for?" Reese said, cutting to the chase. "You wanted me to give you a pep talk and tell you something that would encourage you, so chill out," he said, taking charge.

"Okay, so what you got?"

"Sometimes family is all you got. You and I

both know that until you know the whole story, you don't need to assume anything. If you truly learned from not giving me the benefit of the doubt, practice that with your father."

"Alright, I'll try. I'll call you later," I said as I exhaled.

"Text me and let me know how you're doing. I care about you."

"I know you do." I said to him.

Taking in Reese's advice, I needed to confront my dad. Immediately, I went to him. He was getting all snazzy.

"Hey there, you," he said, like I should have no care in the world. "Still got doubts about your daddy, huh?"

I looked at him. There was so much I wanted to say, but I couldn't. How do I get him to reveal he was cheating on my mom?

He came over to me and said, "I'm proud of you, Sloan. When you were down, you took some punches you didn't deserve, but you didn't stay beat down. You found a way to get the truth out there, and your reputation is more intact than it's ever been."

"But, Dad. Our family. I just don't understand why you'd . . ."

Cutting me off, he said, "Okay, okay, okay. I get where you're coming from. We talked about this. If my words can't allow you to trust me, then I've got to let my actions speak for me. I've won the mayoral race. Certainly I can win over my daughter so she won't be suspicious. Come now. I want you to come with me."

"I'll go with Mom and everyone else."

"No, no, no. I need your help. I want you to come early with me."

Since I had no choice, I grabbed my stuff. I hugged my mom before I left. She was so pretty, and I wanted her happiness more than anything.

Reluctantly, when the limousine pulled up, I followed behind my dad and got in. I was shocked when I saw female legs. And the shoes I knew too well. I could have choked when I looked up and saw Miss X.

"Dad, are you serious?" I yelled out. "No way do you want me to be here and see this lady. She likes you. She's been texting you off the chain. Don't you know he's a married man?" I screamed.

Miss X laughed. "She's cute, so feisty and all."

"Okay, Dad. This isn't cool," I said, wanting to sock the crazy lady.

"Calm down, girl," my dad said.

I tried to get out of the car, but my dad pressed the lock button. He told the driver to go on.

"Introduce yourself," my dad said to Miss X.

"Like I wanna meet this lady!" I blabbed full of sister-girl attitude.

"My name is Xeena Sams, and I'm a party planner."

"Oh, okay. Whoopty-doo."

I wanted to ask her who was gonna plan her funeral after I get done whooping her butt. I guess my facial expressions illustrated my hatred, so I didn't need to say anything. She was squirming, understanding I was serious.

"I don't know where all the hostility is coming from," Xeena said, "but I've been working hard with your dad. You're right it's been around the clock, and I have been a little pushy."

"You think?" I said.

"Listen to her, Sloan. I told you to calm down," my father demanded.

"I saw a picture of you two all chummy."

Xeena said, "Well, it has been secretive what we've been working on."

"Working on? You still wanna try to pretend that you're doing some kind of party for my dad?"

"I'm doing a party for your dad and your mom."

"It's our anniversary, honey. Your mom's been there with me through thick and thin." I kept this a secret because I wanted her to be surprised. Thanks to the picture, I had to come clean, but I still think this room is going to take her breath away."

I couldn't believe what I was hearing. We pulled up, and I followed them to a ballroom that was decked out in "Happy Anniversary" paraphernalia. I was blown away by the beautiful silver and black decorations. There was an ice sculpture that read *I love you*. Gorgeous roses adorned the tables. Crab claws and cocktail shrimp were on ice. A jazz band was positioned near the dance floor. Xeena had skills—the place was lovely.

From out of nowhere came a man who was fine. Xeena kissed him. He shook my dad's hand, like they knew each other.

She turned to me and said, "This is my fiancé. He is the starting quarterback for the Carolina Panthers. I'm excited about your dad being the mayor, but trust me. I'm good."

She winked my way and walked off with her arm in her beau's. I felt so bad. I was so wrong. I couldn't believe all that I was seeing. I owed my dad such a big apology. Before I could give it, my mom and my sisters walked into the crowded room. My mom was in tears at all my dad had done to show his love for her.

I felt sick to my stomach. All month I didn't have the truth, and I didn't wanna know it. Everything that had been done to me, I had done to my dad.

But I had learned my lesson. I should have trusted what I knew in my heart all the time.

Sometimes the truth lies within; you gotta go with your gut. Yes, you gotta go with the facts, but when you put those two things together, faith shines through, and your family can survive.

My sisters kept looking at me like, "See, you almost messed up Dad and Mom over nothing." That's not what they said at all though.

They came over to me, and Shelby said, "You've been through so much. We love you, girl. Let's enjoy the night."

How could I enjoy the night when I had almost ruined my parent's marriage? The room filled up. My sisters were great hostesses, but I was far from the festivities. My father saw me sulking.

He came over to me and said, "I told you I love you, pumpkin. Are my actions showing you how much? There's no other woman for me than your mom. I love my girls, and I'm proud of you for being such an excellent student and wanting to be a reporter who gets the truth out there. I'm putting together my administration, and I'd like to start a magazine that's for young people. You all need a paper where you can express whatever's going on. I want you to be the editor of it for me and own it with me. How does that sound?"

"Are you serious, Dad?" I said as my eyes watered. "You aren't mad at me?"

"Didn't you just hear me? I'm proud of you. In everything you do, you strive for excellence, and you hold everyone to a high standard. That's my girl."

I'd learned so much. I didn't think I wanted love, but now I was open to it. I never thought my talents could turn into a business, but here my dad was telling me we could own a magazine together. I thought my family was over, but this was just the start of big things.

"I gotta change, Dad. I gotta be better," I said as I held him tight.

Hugging me back, he touched my face and said, "But don't you ever stop being you. You're my precious sweetheart."

ACKNOWLEDGMENTS

Here is a thank you to those who help me settle for the truth and nothing but in my own writing world.

To my parents, Dr. Franklin and Shirley Perry, thank you for showing me the truth of a great education.

To my publisher, especially, Emily Harris, thank you for a truly tight cover.

To my extended family, thank you for telling me the truth that I am living my purpose.

To my assistants Ashley Sanford, Alyxandra Pinkston, and Candace Johnson, thank you for telling me the truth page after page.

To my dear friends, thank you for showing me truly meaningful friendships.

To my teens, Dustyn, Sydni, and Sheldyn, thank you for telling me what truly works in books and what doesn't.

To my husband, Derrick, thank you telling me the truth that when I get knocked down in my career, I am strong enough to get up.

To my readers, thank you for telling me the truth and letting me know my writing makes a difference.

And to my Savior, thank You for telling me the truth that You love me. Your love is everything.

ABOUT THE AUTHOR

STEPHANIE PERRY MOORE is the author of more than sixty young adult titles, including the Grovehill Giants series, the Lockwood Lions series, the Payton Skky series, the Laurel Shadrach series, the Perry Skky Jr. series, the Yasmin Peace series, the Faith Thomas Novelzine series, the Carmen Browne series, the Morgan Love series, the Alec London series, and the Beta Gamma Pi series. Mrs. Moore is a motivational speaker who enjoys encouraging young people to achieve every attainable dream. She lives in the greater Atlanta area with her husband, Derrick, and their three children. Visit her website at www.stephanieperrymoore.com.

THE **SHARP** SISTERS

Make Something
of It

STEPHANIE PERRY MOORE

Better Than
Picture Perfect

STEPHANIE PERRY MOORE

Turn Up
for Real

STEPHANIE PERRY MOORE

Truth and
Nothing But

STEPHANIE PERRY MOORE

Icing on the Cake

STEPHANIE PERRY MOORE